American Mail-Order Brides Series
Book 13

Alice

Bride of Rhode Island

By

Kristy McCaffrey

Books by Kristy McCaffrey

Wings of the West series
The Wren
The Dove
The Sparrow
The Blackbird
The Bluebird
Echo of the Plains (A Novella)

Stand-Alone Novels
Into The Land Of Shadows

Long Novellas
Alice: Bride of Rhode Island

Short Novellas
The Crow and the Coyote
The Crow and the Bear
Canyon Crossing
Lily and Mesquite Joe
A Westward Adventure

What readers are saying about ALICE ~

Dedication

My sincere gratitude to Kirsten Osbourne for inviting me to participate in such a tremendous project. I'm not sure any of us knew what we were getting into when we signed up, but we all weathered the ups and downs and can now see the light at the end of a very crowded tunnel (we had 45 authors trying to keep the facts straight while also flexing our creative muscles—no easy task).

And a warm thanks to my smaller collaborative group— Kit Morgan, Ashley Merrick, Hildie McQueen, Kristin Holt and Madison Johns. I promise not to bug any of you for more snippets from your stories.

Prologue

Lawrence, Massachusetts
Early October 1890

Alice paced near the tiny fireplace, female chatter from the kitchen beckoning. Making up her mind, she moved to the entrance where her friends were preparing supper.

"I have a dilemma," she announced.

Judith looked up from the table, blowing wisps of reddish brown hair from her face as she ceased the chopping of two large heads of cabbage. They'd been lucky to purchase them with the rationing of funds from Lottie's betrothed. Samuel Cooke had kept them fed when few resources were left to them; Lottie was fortunate to have found a good man.

Beth stopped at the edge of the table, the pot in her hand poised mid-air. "What's wrong, Alice?"

1

"I need to make a decision. I need everyone's help." Alice held out a letter.

Leora gasped. "Did you get a response from Mr. Hughes?"

Alice shook her head.

Leora crossed the room, took the missive from Alice, and began reading it. Finally, she raised her gaze, her dark eyes pools of concern. "I don't understand. Who is Frank Martel?"

"I received this letter nearly a week ago," Alice said. "He learned of our predicament through business channels and sought me out. I've yet to hear from Mr. Hughes in Iowa." Alice paused, seeking to quiet her nerves. She was both distressed and excited. Taking a deep breath, she continued, "In fact, I'm beginning to wonder if I ever will. And this Mr. Martel shows great promise."

Judith frowned. "Has he proposed?"

Alice plastered a half-smile onto her lips. "Yes."

Silence engulfed the room.

"This sounds very untoward," Leora said quietly.

"I know what you're thinking. I thought the very same thing. So I took the letter to Miss McDaniel." Roberta McDaniel had been their manager at the Brown Textile Mill until it had burned down a month ago. In her efforts to help all the unmarried women in her employ, she'd encouraged them to consider the possibility of becoming mail-order brides. To that end, she'd instructed the girls to choose a husband from the *Grooms' Gazette*, an advertisement of prospective grooms. "She contacted the matchmaker responsible for her sister's happy union — I believe her name is Elizabeth Miller — and they both investigated. Frank Martel passed inspection."

"Why would you change your mind?" Beth asked. "You liked that Mr. Hughes. I think you should wait."

"How much longer can *any* of us delay?" Alice asked, panic rising in her voice. "We're running out of money. In no time at all, we won't be able to put food on the table. If I accept, it not only helps me, but all of you. The less people in the house, the better."

If only the process had moved as quickly as it had for Lessie and Josie. The twins had found grooms in lightning speed, leaving so quickly for Utah Territory that Alice hadn't had a chance to say farewell.

Leora placed an arm around Alice. "We'll get by somehow. Please don't rush into this on our account."

The girls nodded in agreement.

After the factory fire, Alice hadn't been able to pay for the room she rented in a meager apartment of an elderly couple. They hadn't wanted to evict her, but they'd had no choice. Had Leora and her sister Lottie not taken Alice into their small home along with Judith and Beth—Alice would have faced the very real possibility of begging on the street.

Alice fought back tears. It was bad enough that Lottie was already gone. Despite the cramped conditions of their living situation, her absence left a gaping emptiness. Soon they would each be on their way to a new life with a new husband. Alice tried not to imagine how much she would miss them. She'd found true friends here.

"Wait a moment." Leora glanced at the letter again. "Does this Mr. Martel live in Rhode Island?"

A genuine smile spread on Alice's face. "Yes." She felt almost giddy about the prospect.

"That's why you want this?" Leora grabbed Alice's hand and squeezed gently. "You wish to go home?"

"I can't deny that it tugs at me in a way I had no idea it would."

"But what about your stepfather?" Beth asked.

With blonde tresses and similar features, she and Beth were sometimes mistaken for sisters. But her closest friend engaged life with a feisty demeanor that eluded Alice. More than once she had wished she was more like her.

Alice had fled Newport and her stepfather, Daniel Endicott, to live a life independent from his control. It had been difficult these past weeks not to write to him and request help. His wealth would have alleviated so many issues for the girls, but the price would have been Alice's total acquiescence. They all knew that and had forbidden her to even consider it.

"Frank Martel lives in Tiverton, a good distance from Newport," Alice replied. "It's unlikely I'd ever cross paths with my stepfather. And besides, I'd be married. There'd be nothing he could do to me. Also, Mr. Martel is a fisherman, just like my papa was so many years ago. When I was a child, Papa took me to Tiverton. It just seems like this was all meant to be." Alice bit her lip. "What do you all think?"

Judith stood and hugged Alice. "It must be fate."

They rocked back and forth, laughing. Beth soon joined in, despite her obvious reservations.

When Alice stood back, she caught Leora's somber expression.

"I'm happy for you," Leora said. "Truly I am. But promise me you'll be safe. Write to us. If he turns out to have misrepresented his situation, then leave immediately. If it comes down to it, all of us will ask *our* new husbands to find a groom for you."

Everyone nodded.

It had been years since Alice had had this feeling of love and support, before she'd lost her mother, before her mama had remarried a man who had purported to support the memory of her father but hadn't.

Alice looked, one by one, at her friends. "I'm going to miss each of you so much."

"I'll tell you what I'm *not* going to miss," Judith said, wrinkling her nose, "and that's Beth's cabbage soup."

Beth sighed. "To be truthful, I'd be happy to never eat cabbage soup again for the rest of my life. But right now, I'm hungry, so we had best set it to simmer." She began scooping the cabbage pieces from the table and placing them into the pot.

Alice settled herself at the table with Judith and helped her to knead dough for tomorrow's bread while Leora placed the already-risen dough into the cast-iron oven. As they always did, they shared news of fellow factory girls who'd received letters from potential grooms while they reflected on whether the matches would be good ones and marveled at how far some of them would travel to have a hearth they would be able to call their own.

It was truly one of the happiest moments of Alice's life.

* * * *

Alice folded her cotton work blouses and skirts and placed them into her satchel, atop the one fancy gown she'd brought from Newport. She'd never worn it while in Lawrence, but Beth had recently borrowed it for an evening with her potential groom George Montgomery. Her friend had looked stunning and Alice was glad she'd thought to bring it.

Nerves fluttered in her stomach. Tomorrow she would board a train bound for Rhode Island and a new husband.

I hope I made the right decision.

"A letter from Lottie!" Judith yelled from the first floor.

Alice dropped the clothing and bolted from the tiny bedroom she shared with Beth then ran down the narrow staircase. Beth and Leora were already seated in the kitchen so Alice joined them as Judith broke the seal.

Dear Leora, Beth, Alice, and Judith,

Sam and I have only one day left before we reach Clear Creek. Our journey has been quite eventful. We stopped over in Chicago, as Sam said we would, and took in some sights, including that of our former employer, Bob Brown! I cannot begin to describe my shock when I saw him in the very hotel we were staying! Unfortunately, my new husband forbade me to pursue any sort of contact, so you can imagine my disappointment. Do not despair, Sam was kind enough to offer to help me discover what happened the day of the fire, but he won't let me pursue it by myself any longer. I'll send you what information he is able to glean.

In the meantime, I hope you are all doing well. Leora, I'm sure you are preparing to leave for California, as are you, Alice and Judith. I hope you find much happiness with your new husbands. And Beth, my guess is that, by now, you've heard back from your gentleman. I can't wait to hear about him.

All my love,
Lottie

"She sounds as if she's doing well," Judith remarked, grinning.

Leora knitted her brow. "But she just can't let go of the fact that Mr. Brown might've burned down his own factory."

Alice stood and retrieved the coffeepot from the stove then refilled everyone's half-empty cups. "She should just let it be, as should you Beth."

Alice worried that Beth's curiosity might lead her into trouble.

"Someone needs to hold Mr. Brown accountable," Beth responded, her quiet voice resolute.

"At least Lottie's new husband has stepped in," Judith added, a twinkle in her eye. "He seems to have figured her out already."

Alice laughed. She wondered if Frank Martel would prove to be just as well-suited to her.

1

Tiverton, Rhode Island
Late October 1890

Alice Endicott exited the train, wound tight with anticipation. Carrying a satchel in each hand filled with all of her possessions, she paused and scanned the Tiverton rail station. Her betrothed, Frank Martel, had promised to meet her.

A handful of passengers disembarked onto the narrow wooden platform and swarmed around her as they filed into the modest two-story building. The unpleasant odor of burning coal hit her, and she coughed, but an even more disagreeable stench of rotting fish soon replaced it. The rail stop sat on the water — she'd overheard another gentleman say it was the Sakonnet River — so she supposed there was much fishing up and down the banks, hence the overwhelming foul aroma. Setting her bags down, Alice retrieved a kerchief from her belongings and placed it against her nose. She hoped that waiting on the platform would aid Mr. Martel in finding her.

Tiverton wasn't a large town. She'd had to travel from Boston to Providence, then to Fall River — only eight miles away, but in Massachusetts nonetheless — until finally reaching her new home. Despite the lengthy journey, the Old Colony Railroad had been prompt; a quick glance at a pocket watch that had once belonged to her papa showed that she was right on time.

Eye contact with several passing gentleman proved unfruitful. None of them approached, although two gave her a pleasant nod of greeting. Grasping her bags and holding her breath against the God-awful smell, she slowly walked into the station building.

In the now nearly vacant lobby, Alice sat on a bench and waited. At the far end of the room a clerk busied himself behind a counter, helping an occasional customer. Across from Alice, a boy, likely not older than fifteen, organized his supplies of shoe shine equipment after the recent rush of customers. The train remained outside and would surely be departing soon to cross the Stone Bridge to Portsmouth, then on to Newport.

Alice watched the boy for a while. She brushed the wrinkles from her clothes...stared at the dust motes drifting through a shaft of late-afternoon light...smoothed back a loose strand of hair. After what seemed like hours, she checked her watch again. It had only been fifty-five minutes, but disappointment lodged like a weight at the base of her lungs.

Mr. Martel must have been detained.

She didn't have much money, but it seemed her only option was to make her way to him.

Checking that her bonnet was snug, she tucked the kerchief into the cuff of her moss green walking dress in order to keep it handy. The snug wool garment had kept her warm on the chilly journey. It was the nicest outfit she owned; she'd wanted to look her best when she met Frank. When she'd fled her stepfather two years prior, she'd left most of her fine gowns and day dresses behind.

She stood, fetched her bags, and moved out of the train station. A striking woman in a cocoa-colored ensemble that matched her brown hair passed by, and Alice's eye caught on the bonnet situated high upon the woman's head. Atop it sat a replica of a bird's nest. A pang of envy sliced into Alice over the woman's stature and easy confidence.

One day perhaps I will have such certainty in myself.

"Miss, could you spare a penny?"

Alice turned to find a young boy, probably nine or ten years old, in ragged clothes staring earnestly up at her.

"You poor thing," Alice said. "Where do you live? Where are your parents?"

The boy shrugged.

Alice set down her bags and considered the coins in her reticule dangling from her wrist. She really didn't have much to spare. It had been over a month since the fire at the factory where she'd worked, and she'd had no income since. Marriage wasn't just some romantic notion for her; she was in desperate need of food, lodging, and a warm hearth.

Miss McDaniel had been endlessly supportive to Alice and the other girls left nearly destitute after the fire, and it was she who'd helped to arrange the marriages. Alice had never desired to wed, especially after her forced betrothal to William Evans by her stepfather, but she'd quickly come to realize that her notions were too fanciful. Her friends had all embraced becoming mail-order brides, finally convincing Alice to do the same.

Even in the darkest of hours, Alice had been determined to never return to her stepfather, despite the financial respite that would've brought.

The boy grabbed her hand and began tugging for her to follow.

Alice attempted to stop him. "No. I can't go with you. I must get to Martel Fishing Enterprises."

"Please come, miss," the boy pleaded. "I want to show you something."

"Toby!" A man's voice startled Alice. "Leave the woman alone."

Alice turned to see a tall, imposing man approach. His stern expression made her wonder if he was the father. The boy—Toby—released her hand. Alice stepped back to let the gentleman handle the child.

"Run along now," he said. "You know better than to harass the passengers."

"Is he your son?" Alice asked.

The man's gaze shifted to her, and she stared into his blue-green eyes. A black hat covered ebony hair, and his broad frame filled a double-breasted sable frock coat in fine form.

He shook his head. "No. He means to drag you around the corner where you'll likely be robbed." He looked back to the boy. "Isn't that right, Toby?"

Alice gasped. "That's terrible. A boy this young shouldn't be living a life of crime."

"Well, be that as it may, life is what it is sometimes."

Alice was taken aback by the callousness of the man.

"Are you new to town?" he asked. "May I help you find your way somewhere?"

For a moment, Alice thought to keep her predicament private. But, truthfully, she could use help.

"I was to meet a man by the name of Frank Martel, but it would seem he's been detained."

When she mentioned her betrothed, the man's expression changed from stern to surprise.

"Do you know him?" asked Alice.

The man's countenance closed down again. "He's my brother."

"Oh, lovely." Alice extended her gloved hand. "It's a pleasure to meet you, Mr. Martel. Are you James or Theo?"

He frowned. "James." He took her hand then released it.

"Would it be too much trouble to ask you for transportation to Frank's home or business?"

Mr. Martel rested hands on his hips, looking a bit stunned. Alice wondered why.

"And *who* are you?" he asked.

"I'm Frank's mail-order bride."

"His what?"

A bad feeling settled over Alice. "Did he not mention me?"

Mr. Martel gave a slight shake of his head.

"Are you certain?" she persisted. "I've come all the way from Massachusetts, although I was born and raised in Newport."

Mr. Martel's gaze honed in on her. "What's your name?"

"Alice Endicott, sir."

She couldn't be positive, but the barest hint of a smile tugged at the man's mouth. He was undeniably handsome. She swiftly shook off that wayward thought. Perhaps Frank would favor the good looks of his brother. If that was true, then she might be fortunate to have strong, healthy children.

"Well, I do believe it's my duty to escort you, Miss Endicott." He retrieved her two satchels.

"My thanks, sir." Abruptly she turned back to the boy; Toby hadn't completely departed. She opened her reticule, dug out a five-cent piece, and handed it to the boy. "Try to stay out of trouble." The lad grabbed the coin and ran away.

Still watching the youth, she retreated. When she spun around, she bumped into the hard wall that was Mr. Martel's chest and jumped back.

"Why did you give him money?" he asked.

"Everyone deserves help in this life."

"He'll just keep stealing."

"Then perhaps you should offer him a job and a place to live."

"You have a far kinder heart than I do, Miss Endicott." He strode away from her, and she had to walk quickly to keep pace with him.

She hoped Frank wasn't as serious and unfeeling as his brother.

2

"What could've possibly compelled you to send for a mail-order bride?" James asked his brother, leaning back in his office chair, letting out a frustrated sigh.

The day had started off bad and just kept getting worse. His meeting with Lillie Jenkins, widow of his friend Stephen, hadn't gone as hoped. She was reluctant to merge Stephen's fishing holdings with the Martels', confounding James. He and his brothers had worked hard at the enterprise their father had toiled away at for years; now, James wanted to expand. He'd escorted Lillie to the train station when, soon after, he'd bumped into Frank's new fiancée.

Frank pivoted from the window that overlooked Pierce's Wharf, a pier along the Sakonnet River. "I'll admit, it was rather impulsive, but it killed two birds with one stone."

"I can't wait to hear this," James mumbled. Frank was *always* impulsive, the complete opposite of him.

"Well, Mary Jane and I had broken things off, and I felt a little lost. I thought this the perfect rebound solution. I wouldn't marry for love, and Mary Jane would realize very quickly that she'd ruined her chances with me and regret it forever."

This sounded like a Frank Plan. James remained silent to hear the rest.

"So, I found out about a ridiculous number of girls looking to marry. I guess some factory had burned down where they all worked, and they were out on the street and desperate."

"Clearly that would make them good wife material," James cut in.

"But wait." Frank moved to the desk and stared down James. "I managed to get a gander at the list of names. I requested her specifically. Her name is Alice *Endicott*. Don't you see?"

James waited again.

"She's Daniel Endicott's daughter."

"That's impossible. Why would Endicott's daughter be working in a factory?" Daniel Endicott was a wealthy man who made his home in Newport. He was also the source of heartache and discord for the Martel family. "She only had a few coins in her purse when I found her looking quite lost at the train station. Which, by the way, was terribly irresponsible of you for not meeting her."

"Yeah, well, I forgot." Frank started pacing. "Look, she's his daughter. I made inquiries. I don't know why she's acting all poor and down-on-her-luck, but that's for you to figure out."

"And why is that?"

"Because I can't marry her. You'll have to."

"You're out of your mind."

"Look, Mary Jane and I reconciled just last night. I can't marry Miss Endicott now. I should've sent word, but obviously it's too late. Besides, one of us *has* to marry her."

"Why?"

"Several months ago, when I was down in Newport, I settled in for a bout of cards, and there was a fella at the table by the name of Evans. Seems he was destined to marry Alice Endicott before she ran off and disappeared. He was so liquored up he shared with the table that she's to inherit Menhaden Fishing Company when she turns twenty-one."

James eyes snapped to Frank. "Are you certain?"

Frank sighed. "Of course, I can't be *completely* certain. Further investigation turned up nothing. I doubt her inheritance is meant to be public knowledge. In fact, I'm not even sure Miss Endicott herself knows."

James' pulse quickened. This was the closest he'd ever come to finding a way to exact revenge for what Daniel Endicott had done to his father almost ten years ago. Menhaden Fishing Company had belonged to Jean Martel before Endicott ruined him and stole it away. Jean had struggled to rebuild his business — renamed Martel Fishing Enterprises — but it had been a slow and laborious process, and he'd never recovered from the blow of losing his business, neither financially nor mentally.

"How old is she?" asked James.

"Twenty. Her birthday is December twenty-fourth. In two months, she'll be in possession of papa's heart and soul. But more importantly, *so will her husband.*"

James shook his head. "There are so many unknowns in this plan, I don't even know where to begin. Not the least, of course, is marrying against one's will. Mine and hers, I suspect."

"She came here. Clearly she's agreed to the marriage."

"She agreed to marry *you*, though I can't imagine why."

Frank moved back to the window.

"Have Theo marry her if you're so determined to use her like a horse you plan to run to ground," James said, but as soon as the words were out, he didn't like the sound of them. A vision of her blue eyes and rosy cheeks popped into his head, along with sun-kissed tresses peeking from beneath her bonnet.

Frank faced him. "You know Theo can't handle her."

James understood what he said, but pretended not to. Their youngest brother, barely twenty-one, was too wet behind the ears to handle a woman, let alone a wife. And Alice Endicott was a beautiful woman.

"She's lovelier than I expected from the likes of that snake Daniel Endicott," Frank continued.

"You seem to be forgetting Mama and Papa's devout Catholic beliefs," James asserted, even though he sensed his life was about to take a drastic change. "Marrying out of spite would have Mama fainting."

Frank paused. "Leave it to you to throw our dear *maman* in my face. All right, marry Miss Endicott, but leave her virtue intact if you must. When all is said and done, get an annulment. No harm done. She'll be free to marry again, as will you. I know you're saving yourself for true love."

Frank could convince a mother to give up her child if it suited him. He didn't lack in charm, an attribute he inherited from their papa. Their mother had always had a soft spot for Frank. James understood it, but it also rankled. After the sudden deaths of Jean-Francois and Ada Martel five years prior, the struggling family business had been left to James to run. He was also responsible for cleaning up Frank's messes.

He was about to mop up another one.

James stood. "I guess we best break the news to the young lady."

Frank grinned. "You don't have to look like you're about to attend your own funeral. Enjoy it, older brother. By the end of the week, you'll be married."

James glared at his kin and departed the office to find his newly-betrothed.

3

As soon as Alice had arrived at the office of Martel Fishing Enterprises, the older Mr. Martel had sequestered himself away with Frank, her betrothed. Frank — with the same dark hair as James but shorter in stature — hadn't appeared too happy to see her, barely shaking her hand. She had a sinking feeling she'd soon be headed back to the train station.

She ruminated over what she should now do. She didn't have enough money for a return ticket. Besides, she had nothing to return to. All her good friends from the factory were in the process of departing for their own new husbands and lives. And besides, Massachusetts wasn't really her home. She exited the stifling atmosphere of the office and wandered down to the stone pier, holding her bonnet in her hand and enjoying the crisp breeze upon her face. In the distance lay the Atlantic Ocean. The Sakonnet River must be more of a tidal inlet than a true river.

She stopped and closed her eyes; for the briefest moment the weight of the past several weeks left her. Seagulls squawked, and a breeze blew wisps of blonde tendrils that had escaped her bun across her cheeks. The odor of fish — thankfully not as pungent as at the rail station — and briny air accosted her, and tears burned her eyes as she thought of her father. Gavin Harrington had truly loved the sea, maybe even more than his wife and daughter.

Into each life some rain must fall. The words of her papa's favorite poet, Henry Wadsworth Longfellow, filled her mind. Well, it would seem her life was drenched at this point.

Alice decided that whatever the Martel brothers had in store for her, she wouldn't leave Rhode Island. She would simply have to find work...somewhere. Somehow she'd get by. She would never return to the home of Daniel Endicott.

Footsteps from behind signaled the approach of, she guessed, Frank Martel, but she was surprised when his older brother James stood beside her and leaned forearms on the railing. In the distance, a steamship called the *Queen City* slowly approached.

"Do you like the sea, Miss Endicott?"

She nodded. "If I'd been a man, I would've worked on a ship. I can think of nothing more liberating than being at sea, sailing to some unknown land. It must be terribly exciting." She glanced at the elder Martel and was taken aback by the contemplative gaze he bestowed on her. The frock coat was gone; the cuffs of his white tailored shirt were rolled to his elbows, revealing muscled forearms. With his hat also discarded, the breeze lifted his tresses with the gentlest of caresses, putting her in mind of a pirate from her school books.

Unsettled, she returned to staring straight ahead before continuing. "Let me save you the trouble of an uncomfortable conversation. I'm not completely witless. I've gathered that I'm not as welcome here as Frank's letters had conveyed. I'll just be on my way, but if it wouldn't trouble you, I'd like to watch the water for a bit longer."

"We've not been acquainted for long, but witless is hardly a description I'd apply to you." He took a deep breath. "It's true. Frank isn't in a position to marry you. He's promised himself to another."

"I see." Humiliation engulfed her. Beth had been right—she should've waited for Mr. Hughes of Iowa to respond. Now, she was left with nothing.

The man beside her shifted, reminding her she wasn't alone. From the corner of her eye, James Martel appeared...nervous. But that couldn't be. He was imposing, stalwart, and remote. A man who seemed shaken by very little in life.

"I'd like to offer you an alternative." He cleared his throat and faced forward. "*I'll* marry you."

Shocked, Alice faced him. "I beg your pardon."

His eyes met hers. "If you'll have me," he added.

Panic threaded through her. She'd been prepared to wed Frank. His letters had shown an earnestness towards her, along with a good dose of humor. James appeared to be the furthest creature from whimsical. Then again, Frank had obviously not been truthful. Perhaps wittiness wasn't a good measure of a suitable husband.

"I'm no charity case, sir. You don't have to do this. I'll figure something out."

"As I understand, you left a situation in Massachusetts that was somewhat...desperate. Do you have family here that would help you?"

She considered her stepfather and his mansion in Newport. "No, I don't."

James watched her intently. "You couldn't go back to your father?"

"My father is deceased."

James raised an eyebrow. "He is?"

"My stepfather is still living, but he and I are distant."

"And why is that?"

Alice stared at this man who had offered to become her husband. He was a stranger. Becoming a mail-order bride was more difficult than she'd imagined. She truly was in over her head. "I'd rather not say, sir. I don't know you."

His response was silence.

"May I ask why you would want to take a woman you don't know to be your wife?" she blurted. "You're very handsome. Surely there's a woman you fancy."

His piercing gaze had her shuffling uncomfortably from foot to foot.

Then, he smiled and her breath caught. He had certainly been good-looking in the stoic stance she'd only ever seen of him, but when he grinned, a boyish, rakish appeal snagged her as if he'd reeled her in on a fishing line.

"I accept your compliment," he said. "The truth is, I wasn't planning to marry. Running our fishing fleet keeps me busy, but Frank was irresponsible in how he handled this situation, and I feel compelled to rectify it."

"You sound like a knight in shining armor."

She wished he would stop grinning, as she was swiftly losing her train of thought.

"I like that," he said. "Will you let me rescue you, Miss Endicott?"

Alice didn't know what to say. She knew the correct answer was no. But looking into Mr. Martel's eyes, more deep blue than green, much like the ocean beside them, fate tugged at her, whispering in her ear. *Life is a grand adventure.* Her papa had told her such when she was young.

James Martel represented a new beginning, and perhaps it wasn't altogether a bad one.

"Yes, Mr. Martel," she answered quietly. "I'll marry you."

4

Alice took a deep breath and smoothed her hands down the lovely gown that Mrs. Irwin had altered for her. The white silk material draped in cascading waves from a modest, high-necked bodice. Puff sleeves adorned longer ones, intricate lace encircling the cuffs and an overlay that covered her bosom. A wide ribbon at the waist ended in a large bow at the back, sitting atop a short train that could be bustled after the ceremony. White silk gloves completed the ensemble.

For the past week, Alice had resided in the cottage home in town of the portly Mrs. Irwin and her husband. The older woman apparently cooked, cleaned, ironed, and essentially kept house for the Martel brothers, who all lived together. Alice had yet to see the residence, situated on the banks of the Sakonnet, but by this evening it would become her new home.

Mrs. Irwin reached up to pat Alice's curls that were tucked into place with pins and a spritely array of flowers. "You're so very pretty, my dear."

"Thank you, ma'am."

"Are you ready?"

Alice nodded, hoping the butterflies in her stomach would settle down. It was November 2, her wedding day. She wished fervently that Beth or Leora or any of the girls were here. Without a confidant to serve as a witness, it was decided that Mary Jane Beckett—Frank's sweetheart—would be her Maid of Honor. Frank would be James' Best Man. Alice soon learned that Mary Jane had no idea it was to Frank that Alice was originally betrothed. James had murmured under his breath during one of the few times they were together this week that she should probably keep that fact to herself.

The dark-haired Mary Jane appeared slightly distracted whenever Alice spoke with her. She was cordial, but it was clear she didn't consider Alice worth her time. Alice wasn't sure how to handle this. She yearned for a familiar face, for a devoted friend to stand beside her rather than the impatient Mary Jane.

The only one of her newly-found acquaintances that she genuinely liked was Theo Martel, the youngest brother. They were close in age, and he was open and agreeable in ways that seemed to elude James. The one bright spot in all of this was that she would finally gain a brother, or rather two.

The more she knew of Frank, the more grateful she was that their marriage had never materialized. He was clever and funny, but their personalities simply didn't suit one another.

Then there was James.

Whenever he was near, her heart set to pounding. She hoped he would be satisfied with their marriage. At the same time, she wondered what on earth they would talk about for all the years of their life together. Whenever she was in his company, he was mostly silent. And the two of them hadn't been alone since that afternoon at the wharf when he'd proposed.

She and Mrs. Irwin left the private room where she'd dressed and came to the back of the church where the older woman handed Alice a bundle of flowers. Music began to play and fill Saint Anne's, a French-Canadian parish in Fall River. It was the closest Catholic church to Tiverton. Mr. Irwin appeared and offered an arm to Alice; he would be giving her away.

About two dozen guests had gathered in the pews, all strangers to Alice. To ease her discomfort at being watched so intently, she shifted her gaze to James standing at the altar, Frank beside him. He wore a dark tailcoat atop a matching waistcoat and trousers, his white undershirt offset by a black paisley ascot tie. He was quite the sight, and for a moment Alice forgot to breathe. He most definitely pleased her in looks, and she said a silent prayer that their marriage would be beneficial to both of them.

As Mr. Irwin relinquished her to James, she looked into his eyes, hoping to see...what? She couldn't lie. She wanted James to desire her, if only in the tiniest way. But his demeanor was impossible to read. He tucked her hand in the crook of his arm, and they faced the priest.

The ceremony was longer than she expected and the kiss at the end was simple, not more than a peck on her lips. Disappointment welled up inside her. All week, she'd contemplated what it would be like to kiss James. Apparently, he hadn't been as curious.

They turned to face the guests, and the priest concluded the ceremony with, "Please welcome Mr. and Mrs. James Martel."

Polite clapping ensued.

James clasped her hand and led her from the church. White, fluffy clouds hung in the late afternoon sky, the bright blue patches beginning to fade into gray. Exhilaration rushed through Alice.

I'm married.

James ushered her into a waiting buggy. As the clip-clop of the horse's hooves filled the air, James stared at the passing buildings as they left Fall River and headed back to Tiverton. The reception would be held at Whitridge Hall, not far from the train depot.

Alice folded her hands onto her lap and sought to quiet her nerves. "It was a nice ceremony."

He nodded, but still didn't look at her.

"Have I done something wrong? You seem displeased." She couldn't quite keep the edge from her voice.

He looked at her, his brow furrowed. "No. You look extremely fetching today."

Heat rose to her cheeks from the compliment. "Thank you. And you, too."

Finally, a smile tugged at his mouth and she relaxed a bit.

"Mrs. Irwin was too kind with this beautiful dress she loaned me. She said it had been worn by her daughter."

James' gaze briefly scanned her attire, but he quickly diverted his eyes to continue staring out of the buggy.

Alice's heart beat a staccato in her chest. *He does desire me.* She was sure of it. She felt victorious, but fear also gripped her. Tonight was her wedding night, and she knew precious little of what to expect. Her mama had died five years ago, long before such a conversation could be had. What little she'd heard had been from Lottie and Judith. She would simply have to rely on their advice. She hoped she could remember all they'd said.

5

James took hold of Alice's hand, now free of the silk glove, and tried to ignore the race of his heartbeat from a simple touch.

"Your home is beautiful."

You're beautiful. He ignored the wayward thought. "Thank you."

Once she stepped from the buggy, Alice craned her neck to view the two-story dwelling, the white facade illuminated in the moonlight. The overcast skies of earlier had given way to a clear night, starlight twinkling as if in celebration of their wedding. James reluctantly released her hand, seeing no good reason to continue holding it.

"And all three of you live here?" Alice asked, her soft voice sliding around him.

James nodded. "There seemed no reason for my brothers and I to leave after our mother and father passed."

She paused. "May I inquire as to what happened?"

"It was a carriage accident, five years ago."

"That sounds truly terrible. Please accept my deepest sympathies." The compassion in Alice's gaze tugged at James' conscience.

He had no idea if Frank spoke the truth about her inheritance, but the possibility that he might own Menhaden Fishing in little more than six weeks strengthened his resolve. The company was rightfully his. If anyone should feel regret, it was Daniel Endicott. James held no ill will toward Alice and was assuaged by the thought that he would behave like a gentleman while her husband. He'd do his best to make her comfortable before divorcing her.

In an effort to deflect the awkward silence that had descended between them, James said, "This area was part of the original Plymouth colony in the 1600's. We believe the home was built around 1750 by a man named Otis Almy. You won't find a better property along the Sakonnet. We added an additional room on the rear west side along with the stone wall and the barn."

She smiled. "I look forward to a full tour."

"Tomorrow perhaps." He indicated for her to precede him into the house.

The festivities after the ceremony had continued late, and his brothers remained at the hall. Alice appeared tired, so James had brought her home—alone.

My wife.

Despite his intention to end the union, he couldn't deny the oddly exhilarating sensation of being officially married. Truth be told, he liked Alice Endicott.

Alice *Martel*, he corrected.

He led her into the foyer, his hand lightly at her back. Her things had been brought earlier from the Irwin's and placed in his bedroom.

"Would you like a nightcap?" he asked.

Tension played across her face. "That would be nice."

James knew he needed to explain the separate bedrooms they would be occupying, but he found himself wishing to avoid a lengthy discussion.

The less entangled he became with his wife, the better. It didn't help that he found her so damn attractive. She appealed to him in every possible way, and standing near her distracted him far too much for a woman he'd only recently met. The light kiss he'd planted on her mouth during the ceremony had left him wanting in ways he hadn't expected.

Veering to the right, he preceded her into the parlor. At a side table he poured two brandies and brought one to her.

She took the glass and smiled unsteadily then drank the contents in one swift swallow.

He watched her in surprise.

She laughed.

He downed his drink. *This is going to be harder than I thought.*

He took her glass from her, his hand brushing her fingers, and tried not to enjoy the satiny feel of her skin. Refilling the beakers with more brandy, he gestured for her to have a seat so that he could more easily put distance between them. Sitting in the chair opposite her, he placed her drink on the table before her hand could get anywhere near his.

"You have many lovely friends, James." The sound of his name all but caressed him. He finished his second drink and poured another, taking his seat again.

Suitably fortified, he decided to end this agony so they could both retire in peace. "Alice, I want to make it clear to you that I don't expect you to share my bed."

The surprise on her face twisted something inside him. "You don't?"

All of the chivalrous reasons instantly fled. She was his wife. He didn't need to keep his distance.

But a vision of his maman filled his head. He wouldn't disrespect her wishes, despite that she no longer walked the earth. If he took Alice to bed, the marriage would be real. And forever.

Once he acquired Menhaden Fishing, he'd have no use for his wife. And he was fairly certain as well that she would have no use for *him*. He was under no delusion—Alice would harbor a deep animosity for him once this was all done.

He would procure the fishing company, but that would be all he took from Alice Endicott Martel.

"We don't know one another well," he continued. "Your things have been placed in my bedroom on the second floor, which is now yours."

"Where will you sleep?"

"The servant's quarters on the first floor, in the addition I mentioned earlier."

"Where will the servants sleep?"

James shifted in his seat. "We don't have any. Mrs. Irwin will no longer be staying here. She'll continue to help us a few times a week. I think her husband will be happy to have her back in their home." The last remark, an attempt to lighten the mood, only increased the confusion on Alice's face.

"But...I don't understand. I thought you *wanted* to be married."

Uncomfortable, James said, "I do. And please feel free to make yourself at home, but I don't expect anything further."

"What about children?" she pressed.

He was glad for the brandy warming his insides, but it still didn't take the edge off her questions. "Perhaps in the future," he lied. "There's no need to rush." But guilt reared its ugly head, jolting him. He needed to escape her company. "You look tired," he said quickly. "Why don't you let me show you to your room."

He turned away as she nodded, her stricken expression more difficult to ignore than he'd imagined.

He led her upstairs, entered his room, and lit the lamp on the nightstand. Then he fled.

6

Alice sat in the parlor with Theo. She stared at the chess pieces and considered her next move, but her mind was restless.

It had been this way for the past week. There had been no honeymoon, just James telling her he didn't expect anything from her. What he'd really meant was that he didn't desire her enough to share his bed.

It bothered her more than she liked.

She was nothing more than a housekeeper. Not that it was unpleasant—Mrs. Irwin had schooled her in the everyday routine and continued to stop in to help, but Alice was confident she could handle the household chores herself. Besides, she didn't have anything else to do.

Why doesn't James want a real marriage with me?

It was true they were virtual strangers, but the only solution for that was to get to know one another. The insufferable man, however, refused to be present long enough for a conversation, let alone a meal.

After supper—*if* he ate supper with them—he would promptly depart, saying he had paperwork that needed his attention. Frank would also leave, to see Mary Beth. That left Theo to take pity on her.

"You're taking a long time on this move." He raised an eyebrow and watched with a youthful countenance. He had the dark look of the Martel men, but still carried a baby face and lankier build.

"My apologies." She moved her rook. "What is James like?"

Theo smiled. "It's hard marrying someone you don't know, isn't it? Please don't take this the wrong way, Alice, but you showing up was a complete surprise. I had no idea James would ever send for a mail-order bride."

James had decided not to tell anyone, not even Theo, that it had been Frank who had requested her. He felt it was better if everyone assumed *he* had sent for a wife.

She exhaled deeply. "Yes, it is hard marrying someone you don't know."

"James has always been serious, but when we were kids, he did look out for me. We moved from Providence to Tiverton when I was eight years old. It was hard settling in, and the other kids picked on me. James was thirteen but tall, so he looked much older. He wouldn't tolerate anyone teasing me. He's a good man, if difficult to live with."

"James told me what happened to your parents. I'm very sorry, Theo."

He stared at the chess pieces and shrugged. "It was James that got us through it. He took over the fishing company. He made it into what it is today."

"Is the business successful?"

Theo nodded and grinned. "We fish the menhaden. Have you heard of them?"

Alice shook her head.

"It's used to make an oil that can be utilized in soap-making and for smearing sheep to keep away parasites and soften the wool. It also makes an efficient compost. We fish mainly in Mount Hope Bay and have a fleet of six ships. James is looking to add more, but what we really hope to acquire is at least one fish oil factory. There are several in this area and it would really grow our business."

"It sounds as if you all work really hard."

"It's all any of us has ever known."

Alice moved her queen. "Check mate."

Theo groaned. "You've beat me again. How did you get to be so good at this game?"

"My papa taught me when I was young. Like you, I've also lost both of my parents. But it's nice to still have a connection to them, isn't it?"

Theo silently agreed. "I think that's why James devotes so much time to the business."

7

Alice placed a freshly-baked loaf of bread wrapped in cheesecloth into the basket, the warm, yeasty odor surrounding her. It sat atop a hunk of cheese and the ham from the previous evening's supper. She went to the back door, shrugged into a heavy wool jacket and donned a bonnet, tying it below her chin. Midday was chilly in November.

Under a clear sky and a bright sun, she began the long walk to the wharf to bring lunch to James, Frank and Theo. Well, most days, it was only Frank and Theo. Her husband had a knack for being absent during her visits.

Seagulls hovered and swooped around her, and Alice took a deep breath of the biting sea air. On bad weather days, she took the buggy. Theo had showed her how to harness the gentle and amiable gray gelding they called Dimitri so that she could go to town if she desired. What she really craved, however, was the company of James. His complete lack of interest in their marriage, *and her*, left her nerves frayed. So, when she could walk, she embraced the exercise with a determined vigor fed by her brittle temper. She'd silently curse him all the way then pause just outside the door, hoping she might see him, hoping he would change.

The Martel Fishing Enterprises building—a ramshackle dwelling sided with weather-beaten shingles—sat at the end of a cluster of fishing-related businesses. Fishing for menhaden, called pogies by the locals, was by far the biggest enterprise, although Theo had told her that clams, quahogs, scallops, and oysters were also harvested during the summer.

Along with running the office, James, Frank and Theo frequently went out with the steamers they owned. On those days, she never saw James, since he arose before dawn and returned well after supper.

She could only hope that on this afternoon her husband was sequestered at his desk, attending to paperwork.

As she stepped from the soft ground to the wooden walkway, the tap of her boots matched the increasing pace of her heartbeat in anticipation of seeing her husband.

Men shouted in the distance. Unease rippled through her as she shifted her gaze to the fishing boats beyond. She set the basket down on the stoop of Martel Fishing and moved toward the commotion.

A sudden explosion blasted through the air, and she fell back. Stunned, she struggled to stand. Racing toward the smoking boat, she bumped into man after man as they yelled and pushed past her. The sight of a body dragged from the water made her heart stop.

James!

"Oh no!" She went immediately to his side as his body was hoisted on to the dock. "What happened?"

Frank crouched across from her, distress pinching his dirty face. "I told him not to go. He was trying to save Freddy from the fire. There was an oil drum..."

Alice removed her gloves and placed her hands on either side of James' head, then beneath his nose. "He's breathing." She checked the length of him, looking for any serious injury. Black soot covered him, and his clothing was torn, but—thankfully— he was still in one piece. "We need to get him back to the office and call a doctor."

Frank shouted to the men milling about, and they soon had hold of James' unconscious form, carrying him up to the fishing office. Alice followed swiftly.

With no piece of furniture large enough to hold James' large frame, Alice searched a sideboard and, upon locating a blanket, placed it onto the floor. The men laid James upon it. She folded a second blanket and slipped it beneath his head.

"Get the doctor," she demanded to Frank.

He nodded and departed.

Alice went to work locating a cloth and basin of water and began cleaning James' face. She unbuttoned his jacket, vest and shirt to assess any unseen injury, surprised by the matte of dark hair that covered his chest. As his wife, she should know such intimate details, and the fact that she didn't filled her with despair.

Please don't leave me, James.

Soon, a man arrived carrying a black bag.

"Alice, let Doc Sanford have a look." Frank gently guided her into the outer room.

She watched the inert form of her husband until someone closed the door.

* * * *

James opened his eyes and found himself in his bedroom, but it had a decidedly feminine touch now. The plain white curtains had been replaced with a light purple lace, the coverlet atop him was in hues of yellows and blues, and a vase filled with flowers sat on the nightstand.

Alice entered the room, and her striped cotton day dress, despite being buttoned to her neck, revealed curves he'd tried his best to ignore. Since the day he'd married her, he'd managed to avoid his wife quite thoroughly.

She smiled, set a tray on the table at the foot of the bed, and turned to push the curtains wide. "I'm glad to see you're awake."

He scowled. "Why do you have flowers in your room?" Had he really just uttered such a silly question? Her presence addled his brain, not unlike the queasy sensation of seasickness.

She returned to the tray. "Although I've been into Tiverton several times, I actually found a delightful shop in Fall River that grows them indoors. I'm afraid I couldn't resist. I've always had a weakness for flowers. It's difficult living in an area that smells like rotting fish all the time. You did give me an allowance and said I could use it however I see fit."

"I thought you might purchase some gowns for yourself."

"I will. But Mrs. Irwin was able to give me several of her daughter's hand-me-downs and I'm a quite capable seamstress." She indicated her attire. "These will do."

Like a schoolboy, his gaze locked onto her attributes as if he'd never before seen a woman. Mrs. Irwin's daughter must be much smaller because Alice's dress was distractingly snug. "How long have I been asleep?" he asked in an effort to break the spell his wife so easily cast over him.

"For a day." She picked up a bowl and spoon and moved to the bedside. "Can you eat some broth? You really need to keep your strength up."

He pushed himself to sit upright. Pain shot through his right ankle. "What the hell happened?"

She set the bowl on the nightstand, beside the flowers, and grabbed his arm to help him. Her touch on his bare skin startled him, and that's when he noticed he wore no shirt. She adjusted the pillows so that he could lean back. Her lemony scent filled his senses, and despite his predicament, he became acutely aware of the two of them alone in his bedroom—correction, *her* bedroom. It didn't matter one whit that it was bright daylight outside.

"Doc Sanford says your ankle is broken. The *Misty Seas* had a fire, and then there was an explosion—"

"Freddy!"

"He's fine." Her hands gently pushed back at this shoulders as he tried to rise from the bed again. "Well, not completely fine, but he's recovering."

Her touch ignited a new kind of panic in his belly. He reached for the bowl of broth and began to eat to distract himself.

"How bad is your pain?" she asked. "Can I give you something for it?"

"No. I'll be fine."

"Once you keep the broth down, I can make you a more substantial meal."

He nodded.

She retrieved the wooden desk chair from the corner and moved it closer to the bed, then sat.

"Will Mrs. Irwin tend to me?" he asked, knowing the question was rude.

Alice glared at him, her forehead creased in displeasure. He stared a moment longer than he should at her flushed cheeks, enticing rose-tinged lips, and blue eyes that reminded him of the sky on days he was on the wide open sea.

"I'm your wife, James." Her back became straighter. "I can tend to you."

Lord have mercy.

He didn't have the strength to argue at the moment as fatigue crept upon him. He put the edge of the bowl to his mouth and swallowed the remainder of the broth in one gulp.

"Slow down," she admonished, standing. "You'll make yourself sick." She took the bowl and spoon from him. "Is there anything else I can get for you?"

"No. I think I might like to rest for a while." *And not imagine what lies beneath that cotton gown you're wearing.*

"Of course." She poured a glass of water from a pitcher and set it on the nightstand. Without warning, she placed the back of her hand to his forehead.

His body jerked in response.

"Easy now," she said, placing her other hand on his bare shoulder. "You don't feel feverish. That's good."

There was more than one way to run a fever. She may as well have just touched him with a hot iron, so easily did his skin react to hers.

She gathered the dishes on the tray, lifted it and left the bedroom, closing the door without looking at him.

James let out a frustrated breath. He could still feel where her hand had all but imprinted onto his forehead and branded his shoulder. What would it be like to hold her, to kiss her, to...

He pushed back the covers to examine his ankle. It was wrapped, so movement was restricted. He tried to shift it, but pain sliced through his lower leg. He was definitely bed-bound for several days.

42

He lay back and stared at the ceiling.

He would ask Frank to bring the books from the office.

With luck, it would keep his mind off his wife.

8

James ran a fever during the night, and Alice checked on him frequently, finally remaining in the bedroom instead of returning to the servant's quarters where she'd been living. She'd insisted that James be brought to his former bedroom. With more sunlight, it was more conducive to healing, and there was an inspiring view of the Sakonnet as an added bonus.

The servant's quarters were small, cramped, and a bit dingy. When she had more time, she would set to work freshening the room, although she hoped to convince James to remain in the upstairs bedroom with her.

The thought made her stomach turn somersaults, as it always did.

It didn't help that the bed she'd slept in—his bed—smelled of him, a sharp musky scent tinged with the sun-warmed salt of the sea.

It drew her like a moth to a flame.

I like the way James smells.

She liked most everything about him, except the way he held her at arm's length.

Keeping the lamplight low, she sat in the chair, reading a collection of poems by Longfellow, estimating it was still an hour before sunrise. James had finally settled into a deep slumber after she'd administered a tonic, and he seemed the better for it.

Truth be told, she didn't want to leave him. Being near gave her purpose. It also gave her comfort.

She wondered if it would ever be possible for them to have a real marriage.

"You're always reading."

She started at James' voice. "My apologies. Is the light bothering you?"

"No. I've slept more in the last few days than my entire childhood."

She smiled, deposited the book onto the nightstand, and rose to check his forehead, but his large hand closed around her wrist to stop her.

"You need to stop doing that."

"But how will I know if you're still feverish?"

"I *will* recover, Alice. I'm no weakling."

She hesitated, but silently agreed and stepped back, and he released his hold on her. In the faint glow of the yellow light, his muscular build filled the bed and beckoned her in a way she'd never before experienced with any man. The way he carried himself, the look of intelligence in his eyes, the strong set of his jaw all enticed her. Sometimes she caught him looking at her, and for the briefest of moments something passed between them. She couldn't fathom why he'd married her only to deny any possible feelings he might have for her.

She sat back onto the chair, frustration welling up inside. "No, you're no weakling." She crossed her arms across her chest, tucking them below her bosom. "Perhaps it's time you shared your history with me."

"What do you mean?"

"Where are you from?"

He pushed himself against the simple plank headboard, his shoulders flexing from the exertion. With great effort she had to stop herself from staring at the sinewy muscle. It was quite possible she would start drooling at any moment.

"I was born in Quebec."

Latching onto the distraction, she asked, "You're French-Canadian?"

"Oui."

One simple French word let the starch out of her. If she'd had one of those fancy fans, she'd be cooling herself off as she pretended to sit sedately before him.

He ran a hand through his hair. "My maman and papa came here when I was still a babe, settling in Providence. Papa was a fisherman. When I was thirteen, he moved to Tiverton to start his own business. When Frank and I were old enough, we began working with him. Theo didn't really get involved until after they were gone."

"You must miss them terribly."

His countenance softened. "I do."

"From the sound of it, you've done a wonderful job with the company."

"I've been very focused on it for the past five years. I was only twenty-one when my folks passed, but I feel as if I've aged a quarter century since."

Alice sensed the weight he carried and wanted to reach out, to touch him, to reassure him that he was no longer alone. But she kept her hands clasped in her lap.

"How is it that you became Daniel Endicott's step-daughter?" he asked.

The edge in James' voice snagged her attention. "Do you know him?"

"A bit. Our businesses overlap."

Apprehension washed over her. Would her path cross her stepfather's despite every effort she'd made to distance herself from him? She sought to steady her nerves. She was married now. Daniel Endicott could no longer force her hand.

James raised an eyebrow. "So, what happened?"

She took a deep breath. "Daniel Endicott and my father were friends—Daniel was his attorney. When my father died, Daniel began to manage all my father's business affairs. I never did quite understand how or why he did this. A year later, he convinced my mother to marry him. Then, he adopted me, and to my surprise, my mother agreed. Neither of us was very happy, though. I misbehaved and was soon shipped off to boarding school."

"I had no idea you harbor such a rebellious spirit."

"There's much you don't know about me."

James flashed a grin at her, and her heart skipped a beat.

"I was eleven years old when my father was lost at sea," she continued. "It's rather ironic, actually, because the sea was his life. Gavin Harrington was most at home on a ship."

"Gavin Harrington was your father?"

She nodded.

"His exploits during the Civil War were well known," he said, his voice filled with reverence.

"What are you talking about?"

"Do you not know?"

She shook her head.

"He was one of the most successful privateers who serviced the Union in blockading the South. My papa knew him and spoke of him with admiration. In fact, they were to go into business together before your father died."

"Truly? What happened?"

James narrowed his gaze. "Daniel Endicott didn't honor the deal." The flash of steely resolve unsettled Alice.

"I'm not surprised," she answered quietly. She had little love for her stepfather.

"I take it you don't have much knowledge of what your father left behind at his death."

"No. I was young. Mama handled everything. And now..." She stared out the window.

"Is your mother still living?"

She brought her attention back to James. "No. Five years ago she died from consumption. I was away at school at the time and never had the opportunity to say goodbye."

James went silent for a time, then finally said, "Did you run away from Daniel Endicott? Is that why you were working in that factory? Is that why you agreed to become a mail-order bride?"

Alice hesitated. "I don't want Daniel Endicott to run my life. I want to be the master of my own journey."

"Agreeing to become a stranger's wife is hardly a way to forge your independence."

"Maybe not." A sudden flare of composure overtook her. "Are you a good man, James? Will you mistreat me?"

"No, Alice, I won't mistreat you. Daniel Endicott can't touch you while you're my wife."

His emphatic answer calmed her, but something about it also troubled her. *'...while you're my wife.'* She didn't like the implication.

Early-morning light filtered into the room, ending the intimacy of their conversation.

She stood. "Let me make you breakfast. Would you like a poached egg and a piece of toast?"

"That would be nice."

"Frank brought home a bag of oranges. I'll squeeze fresh juice for you."

"You're going to spoil me."

If I do, will you want me as a true wife?

The longing for something real and lasting pierced her. She fled to the hall before James could see the look of despair on her face.

9

"No." James set his jaw.

"Why?" Frank argued.

"Alice left Daniel Endicott on purpose. I won't force her back into his life."

Frank leaned forward in the chair that Alice normally occupied. "How will you get your hands on her inheritance if Endicott doesn't know you're her husband?"

"We're not entirely certain there *is* an inheritance." James still lay in bed. It had been three days and he was restless. "I've been making discreet inquiries, but so far nothing."

"All the more reason to stir the pot. It's just a social gathering. At his house, no less. It's perfect. I've already secured an invitation for you. You simply bring your wife along. You don't even have to tell her."

"Do you really think Endicott would let a Martel through his front door?"

Frank smiled, a wicked gleam in his eye. "You'll be going as Mr. and Mrs. Marsh from Boston."

"And what do you expect will happen?" James countered, irritated. He really needed to get up and move about. While being cooped up with Alice had its benefits, it had also created a tension between them — a longing that was fast proving to be a damn frustration. He knew she felt it. And God knew, the more time he spent with her, the more agitated he became.

He'd married her to gain an advantage over Daniel Endicott, to right the many wrongs that had befallen the Martel family because of him. He had no qualms pursuing this course of action. But compromising Alice was untenable to him. She deserved better. Gavin Harrington's daughter merited a man who would love and cherish her, not one who would marry her to gain access to her stepfather. As soon as the business with the inheritance could be handled, James would let her go.

Frank reclined in the chair, stretching his legs and crossing his arms. Having come straight from a day on one of their steamships, the *Three Brothers,* his sweat-soaked shirt, suspenders, and stained wool trousers smelled of fish. It amused James to imagine Alice's reaction when she came across Frank's stench. Her vase of flowers on the nightstand did little to mask it.

"Endicott will know you've got his daughter," Frank answered. "It'll give you leverage. And it'll scare him too, which he more than deserves. It's high time he knows that messing with a Martel was a bad idea."

Frank was right. Jean and Ada Martel had died in a carriage accident, the cause lurking like a fishing net dredging the sea floor. The official conclusion had been that Jean Martel had been drunk, a state in which he'd frequently been found in the years after his ruin by

Endicott. But both James and Frank suspected that Endicott may have had a hand in it. Unfortunately, nothing could be proven.

Frank sighed and ran a hand through his dark hair. "You don't love Alice, so why do you care if she's upset? As soon as this is done, you can divorce her and get on with your life. It's what I'd planned to do when I initially sent for her anyway. You can still live your dream of sailing into the beyond on one of your ships."

James brooded. "I'd never abandon the family or the business." Did that include Alice?

"Will you at least *consider* attending the party?"

"I'll think about it," he finally conceded.

"Don't think too long. It's a Christmas party, set for December 12. You'll need to depart soon if you want to make the journey to Newport without too much hassle. You could tell Alice it's a belated honeymoon."

James swore under his breath as Frank left the room. A honeymoon implied marital relations. That was exactly what James had been trying to avoid these past few weeks. And he wasn't keen about lying to Alice.

You're already misleading her.

He needed to stop the sentiment seeping into him. He hadn't desired to get married. He'd simply saved Frank's hide and Alice's difficult predicament. He didn't owe her anything, except that she leave the marriage as unscathed as when she entered it. In return, he'd take back Menhaden Fishing, his papa's heart and soul. Perhaps Frank was right. The sooner this business with Endicott could be addressed, the sooner he and Alice could get on with their lives.

* * * *

Alice entered James' room, carrying clean linens, and tried to ignore his stewing temperament.

"I want to get out of bed," he said.

"I agree. It's time I freshened the coverings." She set down her bundle and came to the bedside.

James pushed the blanket away and swung his legs to the floor. Alice pretended that his near state of nakedness didn't affect her at all. Since he seemed determined to stand, she wedged herself in the crook of his shoulder to allow him to lean on her.

"I'm not an invalid," he huffed.

She stood her ground. "No, but you certainly are stubborn. Where is it you're planning to go?"

"Downstairs."

"Frank did procure crutches for you. They're in the parlor."

His arm came around her and she wrapped hers around his waist, enjoying the feel of his bare skin.

"But perhaps you should dress before you make your way back into the world," she added. She'd never been this close to him before, and the contact brought a flush of heat to her face.

"Fine."

"Do you need assistance?"

"No."

"I've placed items in the dresser for you. If you can stand, I'll leave you to it."

He nodded.

Reluctantly she separated herself from him, continuing to grasp his arm until she was forced to release the contact.

"I've decided that we'll go to Newport for our honeymoon."

Alice's gaze snapped to his, but his eyes were elsewhere as he braced a hand on the wall at the head of the bed. His lithe frame and muscled torso briefly distracted her.

"Truly?" she asked.

"Yes. In ten days' time. My ankle should be better by then. You should acquire more gowns, at least two fancy ones. We may attend a Christmas party or two."

Elation and apprehension settled in her chest. Did a honeymoon mean that James sought to spend more time with her? In the same instance, she dreaded such a journey. She had grown up in Newport—it was her home—but when she'd fled her stepfather she'd accepted that she would never return.

"That sounds delightful," she murmured.

His eyes came to hers, but they held no warmth or understanding.

"I'll meet you downstairs," she said and left the room, deciding that he could fend for himself.

Alice entered the parlor and sat down, seeking to calm her nerves. To distract herself, she pulled a letter that had arrived earlier from her apron pocket. It was from Judith.

My Dearest Alice,

I received your letter and am so happy to hear you are well. I am writing you to let you know I arrived at my destination in Wyoming. You can't imagine how things have gone for me. Hopefully when I write you next, I can give you more news.

For now, I can only tell you that upon arriving, I found my intended had passed away. Thankfully, I found a position as caregiver for a beautiful baby girl.

It could be that I may have to marry the father, since I live at the house and he is single.

Sean Montgomery is a good man. He is responsible and very respectful. However, it is not right for me to continue to live in his house without being married. His sister is pushing us to wed, and to be honest, I am not opposed, as I find him very handsome.

Once I have more news, I will write you. Know that you are always in my thoughts.

With Love,
Judith Murphy

Alice thought of Judith's predicament, not unlike her own. Alice hadn't married her intended, and now neither would her friend. She said a silent prayer that Judith's situation would prove far better than hers.

* * * *

James watched Alice leave, her lemon scent clinging to him. He'd never envisioned marriage was such a difficult endeavor. When she'd wrapped her arms around him, all he could think of was folding her against him with nothing between them. For a brief, insane moment he couldn't remember why he was staying away from his bride.

Damn.

He hadn't missed the anxiety that pinched her features at the mention of a trip to Newport. He hoped she would understand when he took her to Daniel Endicott's house that he'd protect her.

Daniel Endicott would never hurt a Martel again. And, at least for now, Alice was a Martel.

10

The trip to Newport, while not far, still took the better part of the day. The train, along with carriage rides from the Martel home and to the hotel, left Alice weary by the time she and James arrived at the Ocean House on Touro Street in the early evening.

Because her stepfather maintained a mansion in town, she'd never been to this establishment. Her eyes widened as the buggy stopped at the entrance and James escorted her to the sidewalk.

"This is a lovely hotel, James. Gothic Revival, I believe."

"You've stayed here before?" He presented his arm, and she tucked her gloved hand into it.

"No. But architecture was offered as a course of study at the boarding school I attended. I found it fascinating."

They took the steps to enter the grandiose structure, James walking with only a slight limp. "I had no idea you were so well-educated."

"My stepfather meant to merely send me away, but he inadvertently opened my eyes to the world beyond." Feeling peevish from fatigue, Alice held back adding: *And if you bothered to speak with me on occasion, dear husband, you might come to know me better.*

Although she and James had been forced into close proximity due to his injury, there hadn't been as big a change in their relationship as she'd hoped. Once he'd started moving about, he'd returned to the servant's quarters, and she was once again alone in the upstairs bedroom. Still, there'd been limited but pleasant conversation because he'd been forced to take more meals with her.

He'd said this was a honeymoon — of sorts — but based on his behavior, Alice had her doubts. Added to that aggravation was also a growing trepidation. As the date of their trip had neared, she'd begun to dread returning to Newport.

But to her great surprise, now that she was here, a tendril of joy wrapped around her. It was her home, after all. Daniel Endicott couldn't take those memories from her. She'd had many happy times with her mother and father. Perhaps she'd be able to reconnect with a few friends. And what about her grandmother? It had been years since she'd had contact with her father's mother, but she should investigate whether Edith Harrington still lived. Now that she was married, family was important.

They entered the lobby, and she removed her gloves while James went to procure the rooms, for surely she would have her own accommodations. Her husband didn't share her bed in their own home, why would he here?

She untied the ribbon at her chin and carefully lifted the promenade bonnet from her head as she took in the elegant fashions of several ladies that passed by. Its straw construction was too simple for the surroundings. But Alice had always preferred simplicity in the designs she wore. Her mother had always tried to dress her in more frippery than she could stomach, and they'd clashed many times over it.

A sudden rush of sadness filled her.

What I wouldn't give to see Mama again.

To distract herself, she took in the finery of the hotel, from the rich Brussels carpeting to the rosewood chairs covered in a heavy satin brocade. Expensive-looking lace curtains descended from the ceiling and window cornices. A large Christmas tree stood vigil in one corner, adorned with glass ornaments and balls in bright colors, tin cutouts in various shapes, and wax angels with spun-glass wings.

Christmastime was a mixed blessing since her birthday fell on Christmas Eve. When she was young, it had always been a joyful time, but after her papa had died and her mama remarried Daniel Endicott, there hadn't been much merriment to be found.

For a moment Alice envisioned an idyllic scene before a roaring fire at the Martel home, James beside her, and children...

She wondered what gift she could possibly get for her new husband.

Perhaps I should break his other leg so he can't escape me.

She chided herself for the uncharitable thought while allowing a slight smile of amusement to reach her lips. Maybe having a child wasn't such an outrageous idea. The only problem was that in order to become pregnant, a wife needed her husband to engage in marital relations. That much she knew, if not the specific details.

A glance at James as he approached from across the lobby made her breath catch. His brooding expression and strong, sculpted face coupled with his tall muscular frame drew her near like a kitten she'd once had who'd always wanted to burrow under the covers. Alice was more than willing to bury herself in the warm embrace of her husband, if only he'd let her.

"Shall we?" James took her by the elbow and led her to a staircase.

Pride stiffened her spine. "Just tell me my room number. I can find my own way."

"It wouldn't be proper for a married couple to stay in separate rooms." His hand still gently grasped her arm.

While a frisson of excitement stirred in her abdomen, she knew better than to read anything further into his statement. "You like playing this game, don't you?"

They stopped before Room 205. "What game would that be?"

"This farce that you call our marriage." So much for winning him over with sweet nothings and her womanly attributes, not that she had any illusions that such techniques would work with James.

A muscle in his jaw twitched as he unlocked the door, and she sensed a brewing anger in him.

"I'm sorry you're not happy with our arrangement, Alice." He opened the door and bade her enter before him. "But, unfortunately, we will be sharing this room."

Baffled as to why she'd picked a fight with him, Alice stepped across the threshold and once again she stopped to stare. Her temper softened as she took in the opulence of the room. A private parlor contained a settee and two chairs around a glossy table and a modest desk in the corner. Beyond, a spacious bedroom beckoned.

"It's beautiful, James."

"I'm glad you like it. The bellboy will have our things brought up shortly. Why don't you rest and freshen up. I'll return in an hour and escort you to supper."

She nodded, awkwardness overtaking her. Would she and James be sharing the only bed? So much for her willingness to conceive his child. She was too uncomfortable to even look him in the eye now.

He placed his hat on his head, left several bills on the short table near the entrance for her to tip the bellboy, and departed.

Her shoulders sagged, and she sat upon an upholstered chair. She was on her honeymoon in one of the most beautiful hotels in Newport. By all accounts, this should be a happy time for her. But marriage was turning out to be nothing like she'd imagined.

* * * *

James sat across from Alice at an intimate table in the hotel restaurant. Despite the faint shadows beneath her eyes, she was radiant in one of the new gowns Mrs. Irwin had helped her acquire. A modest neckline nevertheless enhanced her bosom, the emerald fabric highlighting the creamy hue of her skin. Her hair was pinned in a simple array, but James had never seen her more beautiful.

"Are you happy to be back in Newport?" he asked.

"Yes, of course. I have many fond memories of growing up here."

"If there's anyone you'd like to visit while we're here, I'd be happy to arrange it for you."

"Thank you." She took a sip of the wine he'd ordered.

The waiter soon brought a meal of stuffed duck with apples and apricots, golden potatoes, and crispy biscuits. James' mouth watered, his appetite in full force after a long day of enduring his wife's company.

It was a double-edged sword—while he enjoyed, and at times craved, her attention, the practicality of putting distance between them pressed on him. He had no idea how he would tolerate sharing a hotel room with her; while it had seemed simple in execution, the reality was filled with more temptation than James cared for. But to have separate accommodations would've created too much talk. And too much risk. If Daniel Endicott did find them, James wanted Alice close.

"How is your food?" he asked.

"It's delicious." Her blue eyes briefly mesmerized him.

A sharp longing to know her—*really* know her—shot through him. "Tell me about your childhood."

She dabbed the corner of her mouth with a napkin. "I was born in Newport. My mother was much younger than my father, but they only ever had one child. Papa was away a lot, since he could never be gone from the sea for long. We lived in a small cottage out of town until we were able to move. I grew up not far from here, over on Thames Street."

"Maybe you can show me one afternoon."

She sampled her meal, pausing to swallow before replying. "If you like."

"Did you ever go out on a ship with your father?"

Alice smiled. "Of a sort. Quite often he would take me aboard and let me scamper about while the vessel was still docked at the harbor."

He grinned. "A ship rat." Having finished his meal and with the wine loosening the tension of the day, he sat back and enjoyed the image of a curious, blonde imp exploring a rig.

"I suppose. I always thought that I'd sail around the world with Papa someday."

"I'll take you, Alice." The words were out before he could stop them.

"That sounds like a lofty promise, James, but I do appreciate the offer."

He supposed he had no one to blame for the empty echo in her voice but himself. The vast distance between them was his own doing, but necessary, he reminded himself.

"Alice Endicott?" A man's voice interrupted the intimacy of their meal.

Dressed in a fancy chestnut suit, a clean-shaven man with slicked-back brown hair stopped at their table. He put James in mind of a stuffy, arrogant horse.

Alice's face blanched and her upper-body stiffened.

"I thought I recognized you," the man continued. "I had no idea you were in town."

"I just arrived today." Her tight voice put James on alert.

"Does Daniel know you're here?"

"I don't believe we've met," James cut in. He stood and held a hand out. "James Martel."

"William Evans." *Alice's jilted intended.* James took an instant dislike to the man.

"Have you brought our dear Alice back to us?" William asked.

"I guess you could say that. I'm Alice's husband."

The surprise on William's face pleased James, since he didn't like the proprietary way the man gazed at Alice. It would do well for him—and any man connected to Daniel Endicott—to understand that Alice was under his protection now.

William recovered and turned to Alice, who remained sitting. "This is a bit of a shock. When did the happy occasion occur?" His voice held no gaiety or congratulations.

She smoothed her napkin upon her lap. "About a month ago."

"Well, I'm sure Daniel must be quite pleased. I wish you all the best." With a nod to Alice and a dark gaze upon James, he left them.

James sat but kept his eye on Evans as he moved across the restaurant and had quiet but insistent words with his companions, then abruptly departed.

James shifted his attention to Alice, who appeared dejected. "An old friend?"

"You could say that. He was to be my husband."

Alice's honesty caught James unaware. He'd really thought she would hedge around the subject. A worry began to gnaw in his gut.

Was Alice secretly happy to have seen William Evans?

11

Alice entered the hotel room with James behind her. Fatigued and still reeling from the alarm of encountering William Evans, she wanted to be alone.

But there was precious little privacy. How ironic. For weeks, all she'd craved was time alone with her husband, and now that she had her wish, all she desired was distance.

She tossed her reticule on the table and began to pace. She simply wanted to curl up in her chemise on the bed, pull the covers over her, and pretend the world of Daniel Endicott didn't exist.

Earlier, she'd had to request a hotel girl to help her dress, and clearly she would need to do so again unless James would come to her aid, but she wasn't of a mind to ask.

How was she supposed to conduct herself with James present? They'd never been intimate.

Frustrated, tears burned her eyes. She turned away so that James couldn't see her face and stared out the window, the streets of Newport bustling below.

"Do you still love him?"

She spun around. "What?"

"Is that why you're so upset?"

"No. I don't love him. I never did. I ran away so that I wouldn't *have* to marry him."

Relief shot across James' face, and Alice wanted to scream. What did this man want from her?

"Did he hurt you?"

She paused, reluctant to delve into her courtship with William Evans.

James moved to stand before her, placing his hands on her upper arms. "You don't need to fear him. You're *my* wife now. He can't hurt you."

She looked into his eyes, deep pools of sea-green in the lamplight, and wanted to believe him, wanted to believe that she'd finally found a place where she could build a life, and not just any life. She wanted a home, and a husband, and children. She wanted love.

James brought a hand to her face and leaned forward but stopped when his forehead touched hers. Her heart pounded in her chest, and she brought a hand to his lapel to let him know that she accepted his overture. His thumb gently stroked her cheek, but for one long agonizing moment, he did nothing more.

You big lout, she wanted to say, *just kiss me.*

She angled her face and brought her mouth to his. He didn't retreat, and, emboldened, she pressed closer. As his lips joined with hers, she closed her eyes and surrendered to the strength and response of James. His scent filled her senses, and excitement stirred in her belly.

James broke the kiss. "Alice, this isn't a good idea."

"Why?"

"Because you're very young, and you might not choose to stay in this marriage."

"What are you saying?"

"I'm saying that I'm giving you the freedom to know your own mind, and you should take it." He exhaled sharply, and his words had been marked with a tinge of anger.

He might as well have thrown a glass of cold water into her face.

"I think I should give you privacy," he said. "I'll get a nightcap downstairs. Take your time with your evening routine." He retrieved his hat. "And you can have the bed to yourself."

He opened and shut the door, then was gone.

Alice remained rooted in the center of the room — stunned, shaken, and confused.

She could still feel the warmth of his kiss upon her lips. A memory of desire began to unfurl in her belly, spreading to her limbs.

He does want me.

She took a steadying breath, buoyed by the thought.

But why did he keep her at arm's length? Clearly, he was uncertain about this marriage. But then, why did he wed her in the first place? She'd been prepared to leave when Frank was unwilling to follow through on his commitment. Why hadn't James let her go? What was to be gained by marrying her?

James' words came back to her when she had pressed him about details of his life. *Daniel Endicott didn't honor the deal.*

Did this have something to do with her stepfather?

Her heart dropped like an anchor hitting the sea floor.

She sank to the sofa to contemplate the ramifications. She didn't want to think that James, or

Frank for that matter, were duplicitous in their actions. Even if they were that treacherous, which she doubted, they had nothing to gain.

She possessed very little. Daniel had given her no wealth, no inheritance, and certainly no dowry. When she'd fled more than two years ago, she'd left it all behind.

If James *was* using her, he had taken advantage and married her under false pretense. But he hadn't taken her virtue. Why hadn't he at least done that? It would have bound her to him. As it was, she could end the marriage now. And so could he. Did this mean he planned to use her and discard her, or was he somehow trying to protect her?

Her head throbbed from all the possibilities. She rang the hotel lobby for a maid's help. With her nightgown finally in place, she crawled into the large, ornate bed and slept alone.

* * * *

James drank four brandies before he allowed one thought of Alice into his mind.

He'd come dangerously close to bedding his wife. He shook his head, trying like the dickens to remember why he needed to stay away from her.

Her soft lips, her earnest overture toward him... James tried to remember again why he was down here in the gentleman's lounge drinking, and his enticing wife was lying upstairs in their bed.

William Evans appeared at the arm of the chair where James sat ruminating.

"Fancy running into you down here," Evans said, "what with your wife nearby."

James tilted his head to look at the man but remained silent.

"I'll admit, I was quite shocked to see Alice here," he continued. "I don't suppose she told you, but before she ran off, I was securing our betrothal."

James frowned. "I believe the *ran off* part should tell you all you need to know."

Evans forced a smile. "Well, I'm guessing you haven't met Alice's father, Daniel. He won't approve."

"That would be Alice's *stepfather*. If he has something to say to her, he can say it to me."

"I'm certain he'll want to meet you."

James took a swallow of the smooth liquor. He stood, a good two inches taller than Evans. "And you're to stay away from Alice."

Evans gave an ambiguous sound, but left with a curt nod.

James knew this wasn't the last he'd see of the man.

12

Alice awoke during the night and heard a faint snoring coming from the stuffed settee in the sitting area. It amazed her that she'd never heard James return. She must've been more exhausted than she realized.

She could get up and invite him to the bed, where he'd be far more comfortable. He was still recovering from a broken ankle, and she could tell that it sometimes bothered him.

Her eyelids drifted shut.

I'll beg him to come to bed tomorrow.

She awoke to sunlight streaming through the windows.

The sound of the hotel room door opening and closing brought her fully awake, then James entered carrying a tray. "Good morning."

She scooted to sit. In the light of day, it dawned on her how frumpy she must appear. She wore her most modest sleeping gown—long-sleeved and buttoned to the neck—and she self-consciously fingered the braid trailing from the sleeping cap atop her head.

James was unbearably handsome in a dark suit and white shirt, his face freshly shaven. He set the tray onto the bed. Atop it sat a silver coffee pot, cups and saucers, cream, sugar, and a plate of sweetbreads.

She tucked her knees against her. "Thank you."

He poured the hot, aromatic coffee into a cup and handed it to her on a saucer. "You were very fatigued. I'm glad that you got a good night's sleep."

She reached for the cream and added a dash to her coffee, followed by a spoonful of sugar. "I guess I was tired."

"I have business to attend to today, but I've arranged for a horse and carriage to be available for you, in case you'd like to go anywhere."

She nodded.

"As for this evening," he continued, "I have a previous engagement, so I won't be with you for supper. You can either eat in the restaurant or have something sent up. Please feel free to rest and relax. I promise not to be out late."

Alice sipped her coffee and nibbled on one of the sweetbreads. James' kindness warmed her heart after his rebuff following the kiss, but the *previous engagement* put her senses on alert. Did he have another woman?

Hurt and resentment filled her, but she remained silent.

"I'll leave you to your morning ritual then." He stood and left the room.

Annoyed once again by her husband's abrupt departure, Alice sat in bed, holding her coffee in one hand and a piece of sweetbread in the other. Her appetite fled as her stomach twisted into a knot.

She knew who she would visit in Newport.

* * * *

James left the hotel room and Alice, settling his hat atop his head. He'd never seen her more enticing than now, her sleepy countenance drawing his attention even more than the bit of bosom she'd revealed the previous night in the lovely green gown she'd worn. At least this morning she'd been covered in a nightgown that hid her inevitably fine figure, one that he tried his best to ignore.

Glad for the diversion of business, he had three appointments today in Newport — two concerned the possible purchase of a new schooner for his fleet, and the third was with Lillie Jenkins, the widowed wife of his good friend Stephen. They'd already had a preliminary meeting in Tiverton several weeks prior, regarding the collaboration of their companies — in fact, it was the very day he'd met Alice at the train station, having escorted Lillie for her return to Newport. Now that she'd had time to consider his proposal, he hoped she would see the benefit to both of them.

In the evening was the Christmas party at Daniel Endicott's home. James had decided during the night, while he slumbered uncomfortably on a sofa mere feet from the sleeping form of his beautiful wife, that he wouldn't take her to such an event, Frank be damned. James could play his hand just fine with Endicott without putting Alice through any undue discomfort.

* * * *

Alice scooped her red plaid skirt with one hand and stepped from the carriage into a brisk December wind, gray skies threatening rain or sleet. Despite this, she released the driver and buggy, knowing that she could walk back to the Ocean House when she was done. It was several blocks, but she anticipated a long visit. She was grateful that she'd purchased new boots in Tiverton before the journey. It had been an indulgence to be certain — a fine set made of wool gingham with a stacked wood heel. The best part was the cream cotton twill lining that felt like butter on her feet. Walking would be no hardship, even if it rained.

She dashed quickly toward the seamstress shop owned by Vera McAdams. A bell jingled as she opened and shut the door. Alice untied the ribbon at her chin and removed her bonnet, then pulled the black gloves from her hands. A few ladies browsed and spoke with a young woman. Alice smiled and gazed at the lovely attire on display.

Would James like her in the pink wool bodice and skirt trimmed with ivory lace? Or perhaps the more modest navy silk day dress with long sleeves and pleated shoulders?

A petite elderly woman appeared from a back room. Alice beamed when their eyes met.

"Alice?"

"Yes, Vera. It's me."

Alice embraced the woman, fighting back tears. She held on, so grateful to see her mother's dear friend.

Alice had been in this shop many times, first with her mama as a child, and then as a young lady, alone. Vera McAdams had offered friendship and comfort after the death of Hazel Endicott, when Alice had desperately needed it.

"Oh child, it is so good to see you," Vera whispered against her ear.

Alice leaned back as Vera's scent of roses clung to her and fought the urge to crawl once more into the woman's arms.

"When I heard you'd left..." Vera smiled up at Alice and gently patted her cheek. "I was so worried about you, but I did get your letter. Why are you back? Are you still working at the factory?"

"No. There was a fire and all was lost." Alice took a deep breath. "It's a long story. Would you be able to visit for a bit?"

"Yes, of course." Vera turned to the young girl assisting the two women. "Betsy, I'll be in the back taking a break. Come get me if you need any help."

"Yes, ma'am," Betsy answered.

Alice removed the sage-green jacket then settled into a chair while Vera disappeared to make tea in the kitchen. A widow for many years, Vera had turned her home into a dress shop to support herself.

She returned with a tray filled with tea and cookies. Her eyes lit up when she looked at Alice's dress. "Why, that's very beautiful work."

Alice had loved the plaid pattern as soon as she'd seen it, and the shawl—draped over the bustle and fastened at the waist—was a unique adornment.

"Where did you get it?" Vera asked.

"A wonderful shop in Fall River, near Tiverton, though not as wonderful as yours."

Vera poured the tea. "Did Endicott buy this for you?"

"No. My husband did."

Vera glanced up, surprise clear on her face. "Did you marry William Evans?"

"No, no. It's nothing like that." Alice accepted the tea from Vera and took a sip. She proceeded to tell the woman everything that had happened—beginning with her flight from Daniel Endicott to her job at the factory in Massachusetts to the fire that left her in dire need of a new situation. "Miss McDaniel really had all the girls' best interests at heart. Becoming a mail-order bride was a perfect solution in so many ways."

"I've heard of such arrangements, but don't the brides-to-be generally travel out west?"

73

"Yes, there's a greater need for women out there. But in my case, a suitor came forward and requested me specifically. And, as it turns out, he was from Rhode Island."

"That's remarkably convenient." Vera's eyes dimmed.

"I will admit, it seemed odd to me, but I was terribly eager to return to Rhode Island. In the end, however, I didn't marry him. Instead, I wed his brother."

"Why did his brother marry you? Is he...unable to gain a wife in any other way?"

"No. Not at all. He's quite handsome, in fact. He owns his own company. He's perfect in almost every way."

"Except..."

"Vera, I have no one to turn to, so I must ask you — is it normal for a husband to wait on the marriage bed?"

Vera set her saucer and cup onto the coffee table and smoothed her hands along her deep blue skirt. Her hands bore dark spots, and her knuckles bulged. When had Vera become old? "You and your husband haven't consummated the marriage?"

Alice shook her head.

"Well, perhaps he thinks to make the transition easier for you."

"But there could be another reason, correct?"

"Alice dear." Vera smiled and patted her hand. "It's not for me to pass judgment on something of which I know nothing about. But an unconsummated marriage is more easily dissolved than one that is, at least in the eyes of God."

A bad feeling settled into the pit of Alice's stomach. "He plans to divorce me?"

Concern filled Vera's gaze. "Does he know that Daniel Endicott is your stepfather?"

"Yes, but I didn't tell him until after we'd met."

"But before you married?"

"Yes, but..." Alice considered the chain of events. She'd reflected briefly over them the night before, but had hoped that she was entirely wrong. "Why would he care if Endicott is my father? I left him. There's nothing to be gained."

"Your husband could believe that you still stand to receive a sizable inheritance."

Alice shook her head. "That's not possible. Besides, I hardly think Daniel Endicott will leave me one penny. And I'm fine with that. I don't want any ties to him." She stared down at her hands. "I'm now Alice Martel, and I sincerely hope to remain that way. That's why I wanted to know if you had any advice about how to woo my husband and make him never desire another but me—" Alice stopped short when she looked up to find a stricken look on Vera's face.

"What is it?" asked Alice. "What's wrong?"

"Martel, you say?"

Dread filled Alice. "Yes, why?"

"I'm afraid you're not going to like this, dear."

13

Vera took a sip of tea, and then another, as if fortifying herself to deliver what she had to say. "When we lost your father, it was very sudden. Hazel was distraught. Daniel Endicott, being your father's attorney, stepped in and handled all of the business affairs. In fact, he had his hand in more of them than your mother had realized. Your father had given him shares in many of the ventures."

Vera set her cup on the edge of the coffee table, then continued. "Apparently, your father had a verbal agreement with a man named Jean Martel to finance his business in Tiverton. I believe it was called Menhaden Fishing, but upon your father's death, Daniel refused to honor it. With nothing in writing, it really couldn't be enforced, as I understand. But then Daniel took it one step further. Jean Martel had a large debt on his business, and Daniel came in and bought it out from under him. From all the reports, it ruined the man."

Alice closed her eyes, her hopes and dreams falling away. What man wouldn't want retribution for such an act? It was all too clear that James had married her to gain access to her stepfather.

"Your mother didn't know any of this at the time," Vera continued. "A year later she married Daniel, for both loneliness and pragmatic reasons. He would take care of her, and more importantly, he would take care of *you*."

What had her mother done? Alice wished she could've intervened and shaken an ounce of sense into her. She'd had cross words at the time with her mama, but they were the resentments of a child. "So she married Daniel to preserve what had been Papa's?"

"In the end, I believe so."

"James is just using me." Alice's voice sounded hollow, even to her.

Vera sighed. "It's quite possible. There was talk of retribution from the Martel's, in the form of walkouts at Endicott's fisheries, sabotaged equipment, unexplained fires. Nothing has ever been proven. Your mother came to know of it because Endicott couldn't keep it from her. I always wondered if that's why they sent you off to boarding school."

Alice's eyes snapped to Vera's. "I really thought I was sent away as punishment. Mama never said anything about my safety."

"I'm sure she didn't want to worry you."

"But I'm married to a Martel now." Panic flashed through Alice. "Am I in danger?"

Vera didn't speak, worry clouding her features. "My dear, I don't know. What does your heart say?"

Alice searched for some tendril of hope.

"You say that James appears to be an honorable man," Vera said. "The fact that he hasn't forced you into the marriage bed speaks to that."

Alice silently agreed, but the connection was all too clear. Frank had planned to marry her because her last name was Endicott. When Mary Beth put an end to that, James came forward. She almost laughed out loud when the thought struck that if she'd refused James, then surely Theo would've been next in line. One way or another, the Martel men had plotted against Daniel Endicott. And while she had no sympathy for her stepfather, she couldn't stop the pain filling her.

She'd been nothing but a pawn to all of them. None of them, least of all James, cared one whit for her.

What a fool she'd been.

Vera took her hand. "Maybe you should speak with him before jumping to any conclusions."

The kindness in Vera's eyes unraveled Alice's emotions. Her shoulders sagged in defeat.

"Do you love him?" Vera asked softly.

A sob escaped Alice.

"Oh my dear." Vera folded her into her arms. "I'm so very sorry."

* * * *

Alice spent the better part of the afternoon at Vera's shop, napping on the sofa, weary and frightened by the possibilities set before her. But, finally, she departed. The sky had cleared, and she welcomed the brisk walk to help clear her head. When the Ocean House came into view, she hesitated, anxious over what she should do. As she entered the hotel room, she released a pent-up breath when she saw that James wasn't present.

She paced, trying to sort out her next move.

Vera had told her that Daniel Endicott was hosting a Christmas party in his home this evening. She had vowed when she'd fled two years prior that she was finished with him. But in light of everything she'd learned today, it was clear that she was in the middle of something whether she wanted to be or not.

If she stood by and let circumstances unfold around her, the outcome could very well not be in her best interest.

Would James truly harm me?

She didn't want to believe it. Nothing in his character spoke to such cold indifference. And the kiss the previous night showed that he wasn't completely immune to her.

Squaring her shoulders, she made a decision. If James was determined to play a game of revenge with Daniel Endicott, then she would be no pawn.

She rang the bell for a hotel girl. A swift inspection of her trunk revealed her goal — the fanciest gown in her possession. The burgundy hue had put her in mind of the Christmas holidays when she'd purchased it. Hoping to wear it for an evening with her husband, Alice had chosen it because she thought it might make her a tad bit prettier, maybe even incite James' ardor with a slightly revealing décolletage.

Now, she wore it because when she faced Daniel Endicott, she wanted him to see her as strong, not a child to be controlled.

Regardless of the situation with her husband, tonight she was Mrs. James Martel. She meant to use that fact to her advantage.

14

James held the tumbler of bourbon and watched the crowded parlor of Daniel Endicott's lavish waterside mansion. Located on Washington Street alongside many other fine homes, the impressive entryway opened up to three stories. Exquisite carved wood adorned the staircase, and the stylized stenciled ceilings spoke of an aesthetic that James was loathe to attribute to the man who had ruined his father. Daniel Endicott must've hired a decorator.

James drank sparingly, not wanting to cloud his judgment. He'd entered the party under the name of Marsh, and Endicott registered no recognition upon their brief introduction. The Martel boys all favored their father, but apparently Endicott didn't grasp any connection. Any exchanges between James and the man since the death of James' parents had been via correspondence.

It was just as well.

Daniel Endicott was known for his opulent parties, and he didn't disappoint.

Like a ringleader at a circus, Daniel controlled the crowd. Not an imposing man, he nonetheless possessed a charm that James knew had to be an act. A receding hairline and thickening middle spoke to his age and intemperance, while nothing could hide his beady eyes, not even the occasional boisterous laugh.

Glancing around, James took in the plush furnishings — a carved mahogany sofa along one wall, an intricately designed oak fireplace, parlor and lounge chairs covered in fancy brocades. Ornate candelabras supported long white candles, the flames adding to the cheer in the room. Despite James' dark mood, it was clear that the gentlemen and ladies in attendance were enjoying themselves.

For a brief moment, James wished that his wife was beside him. He tried to imagine a young Alice moving about these rooms, wondering what her life had been like here. Would she have hidden in her room, reading one of her novels? A smile tugged the corners of his mouth. She would no doubt have been a headstrong girl. That she'd left Endicott proved that point.

He wondered, too, how many suitors had pursued her. Her beauty was readily apparent and would've been a beacon to the young men in the social circles with which Daniel so obviously loved to participate. James scanned the room, irritated by the sight of several younger men. If Alice were here, how many would crowd to gain her attention? How many would attempt to court her?

His eyes settled on William Evans, who'd just arrived, although the man had yet to notice James. The thought of his near marriage to Alice left James cold.

A voice echoed in his head. *You're a fool if you let her go.*

A simple twist of fate had brought Alice to him, so why was he trying so hard to be honorable in a marriage of convenience when Alice had no idea why Frank had brought her to Tiverton? While the situation was most definitely muddled with intention, one thought pricked him.

He wanted his wife.

He wanted her to *remain* his wife.

His course of action in the matter was clear. He'd return to Alice tonight and make her his.

To celebrate his silent promise, he downed the bourbon in one swallow, the liquid warming his insides and reinforcing the sudden wave of happiness. As he set the glass onto a table, a hush came over the room. Glancing at the foyer entrance, he froze.

Alice stood in the archway, adorned in a magnificent ruby gown that accentuated her feminine attributes, her blonde hair swept up into curls that spilled onto the revealing skin of her shoulders. And her bosom...

He moved forward, unable to tear his gaze from her, his body taut with the quickening of his temper.

As he approached, shock crossed her face, a slight flush bringing out the blue in her eyes.

"Why are you here?" she asked when he stopped before her.

"I could ask the same of you."

"This was my home. And you've lied to me."

"Alice?" Daniel Endicott's voice broke the look of fury flashing in Alice's gaze. He stared at his step-daughter. "What are you doing here?"

Her rigid stance didn't escape James' attention. "I was in Newport and thought I should return."

"Why didn't you tell me?" Irritation marred Endicott's features. "You couldn't have picked a more inconvenient time."

Alice's cheeks colored to a deep shade of crimson. "This is my home. I believe I have a right to be here."

Endicott considered her words, then slowly nodded. His gaze shifted to James. "Who are you and why are you hovering over my daughter?"

"I could ask why *you're* hovering over *my wife.*"

"Your what?"

William Evans entered the conversation. "I was going to tell you, Daniel. I met him yesterday, and he claims he and Alice are married."

James coolly assessed Evans. "I don't claim it. We *are* married."

"That remains to be seen," Alice said.

James' gaze shifted to hers and her openly defiant countenance. Dread settled into his bones. What had happened?

"I don't believe we've been introduced," Endicott said, but there was nothing cordial in his comment.

Reluctantly, James shifted his attention to Endicott. "James Martel."

Endicott visibly paled, and while James took satisfaction in the man's reaction, a knot began to form in his stomach. Just when he'd accepted that he wanted a forever with Alice, it appeared that she'd changed her mind.

15

Alice sat in one of the uncomfortable armchairs her stepfather used for conducting business in his study. Memories of the frequent lectures she received from him as a girl skirted her thoughts; the twinge of a phantom pain flared beneath her shoulder blade, a remnant of when her slouched spine had pushed against the open slatted back in an effort to recoil from him.

Tonight, the bustle of her gown kept her on the edge of her seat, and she willed herself to sit taller.

I can handle this.

From the corner of her eye, she saw James enter. She'd been shocked to see him here, but it only reinforced that his goal was clearly Daniel Endicott, not her.

"Alice—"

James was cut off as Daniel joined them and firmly shut the door. Thankfully, William Evans had been denied access to this special meeting.

Daniel came to his desk, his expression rigid. The large stuffed leather chair creaked as he sat. He cleared his throat, and his steely gaze landed on Alice. "What exactly is going on here?"

Alice summoned her anger, the only friend she had at the moment. "I believe it's time you told me what you took from my father."

"What are talking about?"

"When my father died, he had vast holdings. You took control of many of those assets. As his daughter, I'm entitled to them."

Daniel flicked a glance at James, who now stood behind her, his hand resting on the back of the chair in which she sat. "It's a bit more complicated than that, Alice."

"I'll get a lawyer." She swallowed her nervousness over the bluff.

Daniel raised an eyebrow. "I'm not here to fight you. I never was. I know that you and I haven't always seen eye to eye. I've never denied you a slice of what I have. And, to be clear, it *is* all mine now." He sat back in his chair, narrowing his eyes. "You ran off, Alice. I knew where you'd gone, of course, but I decided to let you work through this rebellion on your own." He gave a derisive laugh. "However, I had no idea you'd run off and marry a Martel."

"Martel is a finer name than Endicott," James said, the edge in his voice causing a chill to run down Alice's spine.

Daniel considered James. "That's a matter of opinion."

"Despite all the finery, Endicott, a skunk is still a skunk," James rebutted.

"I will not be insulted in my own home." Daniel shifted his gaze to Alice. "I can see now that letting you flee was a mistake. A young woman can't possibly know how to make good decisions about her life." He shook his head, disappointment all but dripping from his lips.

James swore under his breath.

Alice wavered from the chastisement, her confidence plummeting.

"How long have you been married?" Daniel asked.

"Approximately six weeks," Alice replied, squeezing the words out as her throat closed in humiliation.

Under the bright light of Daniel's scrutiny, she could see the grave error she'd made. She'd entered this marriage blindly, believing that love would find its way past any obstacle. But James didn't love her and had made little effort to try.

"Marriages can be undone," Daniel said.

"It's not up to you," James responded.

"You seem rather desperate, Mr. Martel. Alice, you're welcome to stay here until we can sort this all out."

"No." James' voice was firm.

When James continued to speak, Alice spoke over him. "I'll stay."

Both men stared at her.

"Then I stay, too," James said.

"I offer no hospitality to a Martel."

"Believe me, I take no joy in living under your roof, but I won't leave my wife. Like it or not, she's now a Martel."

Daniel stood. "Fine. I'll send a housekeeper to see to your needs. Now, I really must return to my party."

Alice remained sitting as he left.

James began to pace behind her. "Alice, let me explain."

She stood and faced him, stopping him in his tracks. "No. I understand now what has occurred. You used me to get to my stepfather. I'm guessing that was also Frank's plan, but Mary Jane ruined that, so you picked up where he couldn't. How noble of you." The depth of the hurt caught her by surprise. "You, sir, are a disappointment." Tears formed in her eyes. She swept from the room before she embarrassed herself further by weeping.

"Alice..."

She refused to acknowledge what sounded like torment in his voice. Daniel Endicott might not have her best interests at heart, but neither, apparently, did her husband.

* * * *

Alice stared out the huge windows of her childhood room. It was a grand view, overlooking the harbor. She had often settled onto the veranda and dreamt of all the places the anchored trade ships visited. They traveled along the eastern coast of the United States, but some went as far as Europe and even China. There had been a time when she'd nursed the idea of stowing away on one and sailing away for an adventure, where no one could tell her what to do.

She wished she could escape to the sea, the way men had done for ages. The bold wind would caress her cheeks, the frothy waves would beckon her onward, and the whales and dolphins would speak to her in a language only a special few could understand...

Except for her bags that had been brought over from the hotel, her bedroom remained the same; Daniel hadn't changed a thing. The same four-poster bed, the same sofa where she'd spent hours reading, the quilted coverlet gifted from her mother when she turned thirteen. Should she be touched by the fact that Daniel hadn't erased all traces of her presence? Despite her angst over James and facing the dread of returning to Daniel Endicott, an overwhelming sense of homecoming embraced her. Perhaps the life she and her mother had spent with Daniel hadn't been the happiest, but it was nonetheless stitched into the fabric of her life.

She still wore the ornate burgundy gown. When one of the housemaids had offered to help—a girl she didn't recognize; much of the staff was new—she'd refused. She wanted to be alone.

James was in a room down the hall, at her request. Shaken by the evening's events, her toughness had dissolved once she was alone. She didn't want to face her husband in this state.

She hoped she had the tenacity to follow through on salvaging her dignity and regaining control of her father's legacy. She hoped she had the strength to deal with James.

I should divorce him.

She closed her eyes. Despite all evidence to the contrary, she didn't want to end her marriage. A tiny part of her still wished that James might come to love her. But could she trust him?

Her eyes were drawn to a painting on the far wall—a teapot, cup and saucer were arranged pleasingly around a lavender kerchief. Hazel Endicott had made it many years ago.

Her body stiffened at the sound of muffled voices in the hall—the baritone in particular. *James.* Kicking off her slippers, she left her room and moved quietly down the corridor, careful to keep her gown and petticoats from swishing too much.

Conversation came from the room adjacent to hers—her mother's sewing room. The door stood slightly ajar, so Alice paused, not wishing to be seen. She inched closer to peek inside.

James. And a woman!

Alice jerked back.

The woman looked familiar.

Where have I seen her?

Dressed in a peach taffeta gown with puffed sleeves, she was clearly here for the party.

"You should've told me you'd be here," James said.

"You're not my husband," the woman replied. "I can take care of myself. I'm sorry I missed our meeting today, but I left you a message that we could reschedule tomorrow."

Alice's heart landed with a thud inside her chest. She returned to her room and let the tears pour forth, a veritable hurricane of disgrace and hurt.

Not only had James not told her the truth of their marriage, he also had another woman.

James had married her only because her last name was Endicott.

Sliding to the floor in a heap, she succumbed to the pity and despair.

She hadn't even wanted the name of Endicott. She was a Harrington, but Daniel had insisted on adopting her after he and her mother married. Alice had been unable to stop it.

If she had simply been Alice Harrington, would James have come to love her? Of course, she would never have returned to Rhode Island in the first place. Instead, she'd likely be married to Mr. Hughes and living in Iowa, herding sheep or whatever a farmer's wife did.

She wondered if Beth or Lottie were having such a hideous experience as a mail-order bride. If neither of them had married yet, Alice should warn them now.

Don't do it. Your husband might not ever love you.

16

James left his meeting with Lillie Jenkins. He'd returned to the party in search of a drink to cool his panic over the sudden turn of events between him and Alice, only to be shocked further when he found Lillie at Endicott's little soiree. From the solicitous way that Daniel Endicott had hung on Lillie's every word, it was clear that the man was once again mixing business with pleasure.

Stephen Jenkins had been James' good friend, and when he'd died the previous year from a sudden illness, it had devastated James. Stephen's wife, Lillie, had been shaken as well. James had tried to be there for her, to ease her grief as well as to help with Stephen's businesses, which overlapped with Martel Fishing. In fact, James had offered to buy out her holdings — consisting of three very profitable fish oil factories — although he didn't have enough capital for it at the time.

In truth, a partnership between his company and Lillie's made the most sense, but he was having trouble convincing her.

Now he knew why.

Endicott was laying the charm on, and to James' utter disbelief, she appeared to be falling for it. The man had stolen everything from Gavin Harrington, then Jean Martel, and now Stephen Jenkins. It made James' blood boil.

He stopped outside Alice's bedroom door and knocked. After several long minutes, it opened a crack. Alice looked disheveled.

"Let me in, Alice."

"No. I don't want to see you."

She tried to close the door but his hand braced it open. "Please. We need to talk."

"About what?"

"I know you're upset."

"I'm not upset. I'm perfectly fine." Her pinched face and reddened eyes told a different story.

Frustration taxed his patience. "Let me in."

She turned, leaving the door cracked, and was across the room by the time he entered, still wearing the crimson gown that distracted him far too much.

He closed the door. "I should've told you about my connection to your stepfather."

The light of only one lamp illuminated the room, leaving much of it in shadows. Alice stood beyond, cloaked in darkness, but he could make out her face, and the anguish was like a punch in the gut.

"I imagine you want a divorce," she said, her voice low.

That had been the plan all along...until tonight. "I don't."

Her eyes snapped to his, then welled up with tears.

He crossed the room. "Don't cry, Alice."

Bringing a hand to her cheek, he nudged her chin up to look at him. Seeking to strengthen the tenuous bond with his wife in the only way he knew, he carefully brought his mouth to hers. At first, she didn't respond, but neither did she withdraw.

He slid a hand to her waist and drew her closer, keeping his lips upon hers. She trembled.

Deepening the kiss, a fierce hunger took hold of him. During the last two kisses with his wife — at their wedding and in the hotel room — he'd held himself in check. Releasing his control, he gave in to the need he'd tried his damnedest to ignore.

He covered her mouth fully with his, and she yielded at last. James crushed her against him. He laid a trail of kisses down her neck, intoxicated by the underlying scent of lemons on her skin and the soft moan that escaped her lips. Inch by inch, she ceded territory. Covering her mouth once more with his, he nudged her toward the bed.

"I want to make this marriage real," he murmured against her lips.

She froze, no longer responding to him.

"Alice, I want you to be my wife."

She stepped back, but he refused to release her completely.

"Are you not certain anymore?" he asked.

"No, I'm not. It seems a tad too convenient that you're ready to bed me now that my stepfather has learned of our union."

"I know how it appears, but I won't hurt you."

She raised her face, locking her gaze to his. "You already have."

He sensed the change in her — the resolve and the cynicism. In only one day, his wife had transformed into a creature he'd never anticipated. He knew now that he'd played this all wrong.

"Give me a chance, Alice."

She put more distance between them, and he was forced to let her go. "You have much to overcome, James. I'm not sure you can do it."

He grinned, seeking to dampen his ardor. "You underestimate me. I like a challenge." He'd lost this round, but judging by her response, she felt the heat between them as much as he did. He still had a chance. "I'll be in your bed, Mrs. Martel, because you'll beg me to be."

"Hardly," she replied.

Retreating, he paused at the bedroom door, unleashing his desire for her into his gaze. "This isn't over."

* * * *

As the door closed behind James, Alice stood unmoving, stunned by what had just occurred.

She could still feel the warmth of his mouth on hers, the seduction of his lips as he nibbled at the sensitive skin along her neck. She'd been drawn to him from the start, but this new side of James would be her absolute undoing. She almost didn't care if he had another woman, so long as he'd share himself with her as well.

This is madness.

She'd barely managed to keep her wits about her before succumbing to something foolish, like falling into the marriage bed with her husband. She'd been so very close to giving in.

Enough. I refuse to think on this another second.

She squared her shoulders and rang for a housemaid. Once the bulky gown was exchanged for a nightgown, Alice settled into bed—her childhood bed—with a cup of warm milk and a fire blazing in the fireplace. Drained by the days' events, she fell into a deep exhausted sleep, only to be visited by James in her dreams.

* * * *

Alice awoke with a start, a gray haze illuminating the room as the new day beckoned from the darkness. For a brief moment, she couldn't remember where she was, then the events of the previous day came back to her.

Her body still hummed from James' touch, his kisses, his declaration that he wanted her to be a real wife...but a part of her couldn't afford to trust him. She knew it would be better if she remained a virgin, should he end the marriage. And why wouldn't he? He had only married her to gain a way to Daniel Endicott. And what of the woman she'd seen him with earlier? Were they together? She wanted to believe that what she'd seen was something else, but she couldn't behave like a fool.

Clearly she needed to have a more level head, especially if she hoped to gain the upper hand with her stepfather.

She rose from bed and donned a robe and slippers, then moved toward her mother's painting which hung on the wall across from her bed. As the light in the room grew, Alice studied it. The intricate details of the design etched on the cup were lovely. Why had her mama ever only produced this one piece? Why had she given up an activity that she obviously had had a talent for?

Alice remembered a game she and her mother had played after Hazel had married Daniel. Her mama would often hide notes and treats — and, at times, money — around the house, frequently behind artwork, a secret communication that only they shared. Alice would find them and do the same for her mother, although hers were usually silly drawings.

94

Alice looked at the painting again and wondered if there might be such treasures still around the house. Curious, she grasped the frame on both sides and lifted it from its mount, carefully setting it on the floor.

She knelt and turned the artwork around, and elation filled her when she caught sight of a folded piece of paper secured to the back. Opening the letter, Alice expected to find a short note teasing Alice on her tendency to muddy her boots or to bring a book to the supper table. Instead, Alice sank to the floor at the serious tone of her mother's handwriting.

My Dearest Alice,

I've become very ill. First, I want to convey how deeply you live in my heart. The despair I've felt with you so far away at boarding school has left me lost. I wish only to hold you close one last time and pray that I might have the chance to do so. The doctors have done what they can but I sense this life slipping from me. Please know that I've written to you many times but have recently learned that Daniel intercepted the letters at every turn. I think he believed that your presence would be too much for me, or maybe he simply didn't want to spare the expense to bring you home. However, I fear I don't have much time left, and I don't ever want you to think that your mother never thought of you. You have filled my mind every minute of every day. It is my hope that you will one day find this letter, in honor of our game, and learn the truth.

Now, you must be strong, because I fear that Daniel will try to control your life. It was one reason I agreed to send you to the Troy Female Seminary: at least you would receive an outstanding education and could live a life of independence. Despite how painful it was for me to part from you, I have only wanted the best for you.

When I married Daniel, I wasn't ignorant of the type of man he was, but I hoped for the best. Still, just before our wedding, I made a great scene of securing something of value for you, since he'd already acquired all of what your father had worked so hard for. He agreed, quite grudgingly, to bequeath a company to you on your twenty-first birthday – Menhaden Fishing. At the time, I didn't inform you because you were only twelve years old, and you deserved the carefree life of a child. I regret this. Don't let Daniel take this from you, but please know that you may require help in handling this company. I learned much later that Daniel stole it from the man who owned it. I have only one thought of where you can turn for help.

For years, your father was estranged from his mother, Edith Harrington. As I write this, she resides in Newport. It is my hope that you seek her out. As I have no family remaining, she would be your sole relative. I pray that you can find the peace and love with her that Gavin couldn't. Family is important. And perhaps she can offer advice on your inheritance.

My heart is filled to brimming with love for you, Alice.
Your mother, Hazel

17

Alice sat at the dining table—her stepfather to her right and the odious William Evans across from her—as breakfast was spread across a buffet table and served by a butler and housemaid. James entered the room, wearing his usual dark suit, his countenance remote and unreadable. Alice's heart unwillingly skipped a beat when his handsome gaze briefly settled upon her.

Daniel grimaced as he shuffled several newspapers into a pile beside his plate. "Mr. Martel, I suppose you must join us."

James ignored him and moved to the chair beside Alice.

Then, to Alice's great surprise, the woman she'd seen with James the previous evening entered. Wearing an elegant, pale yellow bustle dress adorned with violets springing from a bed of vine leaves, her pretty features all but glowed.

Staring, Alice registered a deeper recognition. This was the woman she'd passed at the train station in Tiverton the day she'd arrived to meet Frank for the first time. Instead, James had found Alice.

Her stomach clenched. James had probably been dropping this woman at the railhead after a rendezvous.

Daniel stood. "Lillie, you look lovely this morning."

She paused and smiled. "Thank you, Daniel."

"I want you to meet my daughter. Alice, this is Lillie Jenkins."

Alice could only bring herself to nod.

Lillie beamed. "Alice, it's a pleasure to meet you at last."

"Beside her is Alice's new husband, James Martel," Daniel said.

Lillie's eyes widened as she gazed at James. "I had no idea that you'd married. When did this happen?"

"A little over a month ago," James answered.

"Well, my apologies for not congratulating you." She looked at Alice with compassion in her eyes. "I'm especially pleased to meet you now. James has always been a good friend."

Daniel huffed a sigh. "Good friend or not, the man has a lot of gall to have snatched my little girl away from me without my permission. William, move down a seat so that Lillie can sit beside me."

Everyone took their places, and the staff poured steaming coffee and fresh juice into waiting cups and glasses.

"And how is it that you and Mr. Martel know one another?" Daniel asked Lillie, the disdain in his voice hard to miss.

Lillie placed a cloth napkin onto her lap. "James and Stephen were good friends."

Alice found her voice at last. "Who's Stephen?"

"He was Lillie's husband," James said. "He passed away last year."

A shadow crossed James' face, and when Alice looked at Lillie she saw a similar pinch of sadness.

"I'm so sorry," Alice said. "You must miss him very much."

Lillie's expression softened. "I do."

Was this why James had been in a private conversation with Lillie? To console her grief? Or did he have an undying love for her?

Alice's angry side longed to find something with which to impugn her scheming spouse. But try as she might, she couldn't see a hint of anything in Lillie's gaze toward James that would indicate something romantic.

Alice turned to Lillie as plates filled with sweet johnnycakes and corned beef hash were deposited at each place setting. "Do you live in Newport?"

"Yes. Daniel was kind enough to let me stay over last night after the party so that I wouldn't have to return home so late."

"It's no trouble," Daniel said. "You're always welcome."

William settled his gaze on James. "So I understand you're looking to expand Martel Fishing."

"I can't imagine what business it is of yours," James replied.

"Tiverton has never been the hub of the fishing industry," Daniel said. "Remaining there will only limit your reach."

"I now own three fish oil processing factories in Tiverton," Lillie remarked. "And they're doing quite well."

"It's such a messy business, Mrs. Jenkins," William said. "You really ought to sell before it declines further. Get the best dollar you can for it."

Lillie sipped her coffee and made a noncommittal sound.

Alice considered the contents of her mother's letter. If what Hazel had said was true, then Alice had just become a major player in this discussion.

Was this what James was after? But how could he have knowledge of her inheritance? Alice hadn't even known. If she told him, what would happen? Would he seduce her then steal it right out from under her?

She couldn't trust him, that much was clear.

A glance at William Evans wasn't even worth a glance. If her stepfather's plans had played out, she'd be married to him now.

Unwillingly, Alice found herself admiring Lillie's poise and beauty, despite the fact the woman might steal James from her.

Daniel waved off the housemaid when she tried to spoon more hash onto his plate. "I wonder if you'll try to buy Lillie's factories, Martel."

"They're not for sale," James replied.

"Everything's for sale." Daniel settled back into his chair. "For the right price."

"You gentlemen seem to think I don't have a say in this," Lillie cut in. "I'm not so easily pushed around."

Alice sensed the tension from James beside her. Were Daniel and James fighting over Lillie's factories or the woman herself?

"I fear that all this talk of business is boring to Alice," Lillie added.

"No, not at all."

"Well, nevertheless, I'm curious to know how you and James met."

"As am I," Daniel said.

Despite her misgivings about James and his intentions, she didn't want to share the truth, knowing that it would cast her husband in a bad light and showcase what a foolish girl she had been. It would only reinforce her stepfather's opinion that she needed his guidance to live her life.

"I met him while I worked at a factory in Massachusetts."

She felt James' eyes on her as she spoke the untruth.

"He was there on business, and we were introduced by mutual acquaintances," she continued. "Our affection grew from there, and I finally came to Tiverton so that we could be married."

"I understand the factory where you worked burned down and many of those girls became mail-order brides," Daniel said.

"Yes, that's true. Several of my good friends have traveled great distances to meet their future husbands."

Daniel focused on her intently. "But you're saying that's not true for you?"

"No," James said, his voice emphatic. "I knew I loved Alice the first moment I saw her."

A flutter of nerves overtook Alice, and her heart flip-flopped in her chest. She knew it was a lie, yet the words blew through her like a whirlwind, and she couldn't quiet the leap of longing in her heart that it might be true.

"But she was more reluctant," James continued. "When the fire occurred, I proposed. I had no intention of letting a woman like Alice go. I considered myself a very fortunate man when she agreed to come to Tiverton."

"I'm sure your intentions were noble." The tone of Daniel's voice, however, contradicted his words.

Lillie smiled. "It sounds as if it were meant to be."

William rose from his seat, all but snarling. "Am I supposed to sit here and take this?" He threw his napkin onto the table and left the room.

Daniel turned his attention to Alice. "You did hurt him when you left."

Irritation bubbled to the surface at her stepfather's attempt to manipulate her. "I didn't love him, and he certainly didn't love me. His reaction is unwarranted."

"Be that as it may, William is my associate, and that broken engagement was an embarrassment on many counts. You'll have to forgive me if it takes some time for me to become accustomed to you being married to a Martel now." Daniel stood also. "I'd like to have a word with you, James, in private."

James tossed his napkin onto the table as well. "I thought you might."

"In my study then. Ladies, if you'll excuse us."

Before James departed, he leaned down and kissed Alice's cheek, the simple gesture muddling her thoughts and unwillingly warming her heart. How was she supposed to make decisions about her future when all she wished to do was to let him kiss her senseless?

Once both men departed, Lillie leaned back in her chair. "It's rather a relief to have them all gone."

Alice sipped her coffee, unsure what she and Lillie Jenkins could possibly have to discuss. Except for James.

"I'm really so very happy that James has found himself a good match," she continued. "Stephen and I always wondered when he'd finally find a woman who could tame him."

Alice responded with a slight smile. "You must be very fond of him."

"Yes."

"Are you his mistress?" The words flew out of Alice's mouth before she could stop them. Horrified by the desperation in her voice, she wanted to shrink into her day dress and disappear.

"Oh my word, no. Is that what you think?" The look of shock on Lillie's face seemed genuine.

"I...umm..." How to explain?

Lillie sat up straighter, her expression serious. "I've never felt more than a brotherly affection for your husband, I can assure you. Whatever made you think otherwise?"

Feeling mortified, Alice said, "Never mind. I find myself fumbling a bit in my married life."

"I can imagine how difficult it is. I gather you don't have much support from your stepfather. I know we don't know each other well, but I'd be happy to help in any way I can."

The offer sounded sincere but Alice decided to steer the conversation away from the mess that was currently her marriage. "Would you tell me about the factories you own in Tiverton?"

* * * *

As soon as James entered the study, Daniel didn't waste any time.

"You've compromised my daughter. I ought to have you arrested."

James remained standing as he had the previous night while Daniel sat at his desk. "Go ahead and try."

Disgust marred Daniel's features. "What exactly do you want? Because you sure as hell didn't marry my daughter out of love."

"I would never hurt Alice."

"Forgive me if I don't believe you." Daniel placed his interlaced fingers onto his belly. "I suppose you're here for a cut of the Endicott money. So I'll make this fast and easy for you. I'll transfer $25,000 to wherever you like, as long as you divorce Alice immediately."

"I can't be bought."

Daniel smirked. "Everyone can be bought."

"Is that what you're doing with Lillie Jenkins?"

"There's nothing wrong in mixing business with pleasure. What's the matter? Did you plan to marry her too once her husband died?"

Anger flared around the edges of James' control. "No, that's your method. Not every man seeks to gain the upper hand with women." But as he said the words, the truth hit him square in the face and he flinched.

Dammit.

He had most definitely taken advantage of Alice. He was no better than Daniel Endicott.

"You're telling me you've not influenced Alice in any way?"

"She's not compromised."

Daniel raised an eyebrow. "You're saying her virtue is still intact?"

This really wasn't a conversation he wanted to have with Daniel Endicott. "At least I didn't try to marry her off to preserve her inheritance."

"And what inheritance would that be?" Endicott pursed his lips. "You're not getting a dime from me, Martel."

"You just offered me $25,000."

"That deal is no longer on the table."

James temper was wearing thin. "You know what you did to my father. You *will* answer for it."

Recognition registered on Daniel's face. "Is that what this is about? Son, you're sorely misguided. Business is business. Jean Martel knew that. I've done nothing wrong, and I'm sorry that you feel this way. What is unconscionable is that you would use my daughter in your supposed vendetta."

"Alice is safe with me. I'll take care of her."

Daniel shook his head. "Empty promises in my book."

"As I see it, you wrote the rule book on empty promises, Endicott."

And with that, James walked out.

18

Alice stepped from the buggy beneath a hazy sky at the entrance to the cemetery in Newport, her bonnet shielding her face from the brisk wind. She resettled the skirt of the sea-blue walking dress then turned to the driver. "Please wait."

She knew the location of Gavin Harrington's gravesite, having visited it many times with her mother that first year after he passed. But when her mother had died, she'd stopped coming. Daniel Endicott hadn't buried Hazel Harrington Endicott here—something Alice had argued to no avail. She'd only been fifteen years old. Afterwards, she'd begun to feel despair and had railed against her own father for leaving her. She had ceased to pay her respects at that point.

She meant to change that today.

Bundling herself into her wool coat and hand muff, she walked to the end of the road and turned right, passing rows of headstones. The somber atmosphere cloaked Alice and the finality of losing both her parents seized her. How she wished they still lived.

She spied an older woman in the distance near the Harrington grave. Before Alice could advance farther, the woman climbed into a nearby carriage, and it promptly departed.

Alice rushed to a cemetery worker. "Pardon me, would you happen to know who that woman is?"

The man nodded. "That would be Mrs. Harrington."

Alice gasped. Her father's mother. She couldn't ignore the coincidence. "Thank you so much."

She returned to her driver and inquired how to find Edith Harrington's home. The driver didn't know, but he asked around and, more than an hour later, pulled up to a modest home on a quiet side street.

Alice climbed the steps and rang the bell. A butler appeared.

"Is Mrs. Harrington in residence?"

"May I say who is calling?"

"Mrs. Alice Martel. I'm an old friend."

He opened the door and let Alice into the foyer, then departed.

The butler returned. "Mrs. Harrington isn't acquainted with you."

"I know, but it's important that I speak with her. I'm...her granddaughter."

He left her once again and Alice stood alone. Finally, the man reappeared and ushered her into a drawing room. Alice removed her bonnet but remained standing. The furnishings were simple and well-worn. It was another several long minutes before Edith Harrington appeared.

The elderly woman stared at Alice, her green eyes shining from a face well covered in wrinkles.

"Hello, grandmother. I hope you'll forgive my intrusion."

"I thought the butler was lying, but you look too much like your mother for it to be otherwise." Mrs. Harrington entered and sat on the sofa. The butler appeared with a tray and set it on the table before them. He poured dark fluid into two tea cups, then departed. "Please sit. It's Alice, isn't it?"

"Yes, ma'am." Alice removed her coat—the butler hadn't offered to take it—and set it on the settee beside her, then sat down.

"Do you like tea?"

"Yes, ma'am."

Edith folded her aging hands into her lap. "Why is your last name Martel? Are you married?"

Edith's forthright manner took Alice aback. "Yes, newly so."

"Then I suppose congratulations are in order," her grandmother added, her gravelly voice not steeped in any sentimentality. "Did your stepfather, Daniel Endicott, arrange it?"

Lying to her grandmother seemed out of the question. "No, ma'am. I was a mail-order bride."

"A what?" Derision coated her words.

"I was in Massachusetts but returned to Rhode Island with the promise of a marriage to a respectable fisherman in Tiverton."

Her grandmother's composure faltered. "I suppose Gavin would have appreciated that."

Alice was sorry that she'd upset the woman but took the crack in her armor as an opening. "I know it's not my place to ask, but why did you stay away from our family all these years?"

Edith hesitated and looked across the room. Just when Alice feared she'd overstepped her bounds, the woman spoke. "I'm not a perfect woman. Sometimes, in anger, one sets a course, and then time takes one even further upon it."

"Were you mad at my father?"

Edith set her cup and saucer onto the table and smoothed her gown. "We disagreed about his passion for the sea. You see, I wanted him to be a minister. I raised Gavin alone, as my husband had died from illness when Gavin was only a boy. My father was a pastor, and it was an honorable duty for him, just as it would've been for Gavin." She sighed. "But oh, how my boy loved the sea. I can see that now. Back then, I was desperate that he do my bidding, but he ran off and lived the life of a vagabond, jumping from ship to ship."

"I'm told he was a revered captain during the War, that he blockaded the South on the ocean."

"Yes," Edith answered softly. "I'd heard that too.".

"Did you ever come to visit us?"

"A few times, after Gavin and Hazel married, after you were born. But the distance between my son and me was still great. He had little to do with me. And now, I sit here looking at you, and I hardly know you." Her voice broke. "Why did you come here?"

"I saw you at Papa's gravesite earlier. One of the caretakers told me who you were." Alice reached into the left sleeve of her gown and pulled the paper she'd found the previous night. "I recently found this letter that was written by my mother before she died."

Alice unfolded it and handed it to Edith.

Edith's eyes swelled with tears when she finally looked up. "I'm so sorry for Hazel's passing. I had no idea. I'm touched that she would even think of me during such a difficult time."

"I still have the pearls you gave me so long ago."

"You do?" Edith's gaze widened in surprise.

"Yes. They mean a great deal to me."

A warm and genuine smile lit her grandmother's features. "I'm very glad to hear that. I'm not sure how I can possibly help you, but I'd be honored to have you back in my life."

"Thank you. I wonder if you'd like to meet my husband?"

"I'd be delighted."

19

Living in Daniel Endicott's home was the last place James desired to be, but he wouldn't leave Alice. Their belongings had been transferred from the hotel and they were both now settled, albeit in separate rooms.

William Evans and Lillie Jenkins were gone, having returned to their respective homes. It had surprised James to find Lillie here, engaging with a man like Daniel. She and Stephen knew of the history between the Martels and Endicott. Her supposed relationship with the man was a betrayal on many levels. James had thought to work with her on her holdings — especially the oil factories located in Tiverton — but if she merged with Endicott, or, God forbid, married him, James could no longer help her.

Of course, he had his own problems with Endicott.

Word was sent that Daniel wouldn't be dining with them for supper, so James anticipated having Alice to himself. He met her in the dining room.

"Are we to be alone?" she asked, her cobalt gown accentuating the bright blue of her eyes.

"It would seem so." He pulled her chair and she sat.

He took a seat at the head of the table, Daniel's seat. The housemaid greeted them and placed a tureen on the table. James lifted the lid and smiled as the mouth-watering smell of the soup filled his nostrils.

"I do love Rhode Island chowder," he remarked.

Alice leaned forward to view the contents and inhaled. "As do I. You simply can't find it anywhere else."

He ladled the clear broth filled with quahogs, potatoes, onions, and bacon into Alice's bowl, then did the same for his own. An amiable silence ensued as they reveled in the dish.

When satiated at last, James returned his focus to Alice. "Where did you go this afternoon?"

"To visit my father's gravesite."

"I would've accompanied you, if you'd just asked."

She set her spoon down. "That's very kind of you to offer. Perhaps another time."

The housemaid removed the first course, then served up breaded veal cutlets and mashed turnips. Alice took a sip of water from a large goblet and pushed at her food with a fork.

"Did you have your fill of the chowder?" he asked.

"May I ask you a question?"

"Of course." He reached for the smaller of his goblets.

"Are you in love with Lillie Jenkins?"

He choked on the red wine he had begun to swallow. "What?"

"You seemed very upset that she was here."

"I *am* dismayed." He set his goblet down. "But not for that reason. I'm disappointed that she would mar Stephen's name by joining forces with a man like your stepfather."

She pinned him with blue eyes to which he was fast becoming helpless.

Seeking to convince her, he added, "Alice, I can assure you there is no other woman in my life, save you."

With a slight nod she resumed picking at her dinner. He supposed his relationship with Lillie might seem so casual as to appear romantic, but that couldn't be further from the truth. A sliver of hope pierced him— Alice's undisguised jealousy hinted at her weakness for him.

"I also visited with my grandmother," Alice said, her countenance still guarded. "I haven't seen her in many years."

"Was it a happy reunion?"

A smile tugged at Alice's mouth. "Yes. She'd like to meet you."

He took the request, small that it may be, as progress in his relationship with his wife. "I look forward to it." Wanting to continue their amiable conversation, he said, "It must've been exciting for you to attend boarding school. Where did you go?"

He was glad to see that Alice had finally begun to consume her dinner.

"I attended the Troy Female Seminary in Troy, New York."

"So you've been on your own for a while." Having finished his meal, he relaxed in his chair, indulging his desire to gaze upon his wife.

"I suppose that's true." With a fork, she placed a piece of veal into her mouth, chewed, then sipped her water again.

"What was it like?"

"All girls. Very strict. But the location along the Hudson River was beautiful. The campus sat atop Mount Ida and overlooked the city of Troy. The curriculum was quite varied — mathematics, modern languages, Latin, history and philosophy. But the purpose of studying was to encourage us to become teachers so that we might all be able to work outside the home."

"Then why did you go to Massachusetts to labor in a textile factory?"

Alice switched to the goblet of wine at the head of her plate and took a generous drink. "I'm afraid I haven't always had great faith in myself. The textile work, while exhausting, seemed a fitting punishment."

James frowned. "For what?"

"For running away."

Stunned laughter escaped James' mouth. "You should hardly feel ashamed of that. Leaving took great courage in my book. Do you still want to become a teacher?"

"Perhaps." She hesitated. "But if I were to pursue a course of action that truly called to me, it would no doubt be related to the sea. To quote my favorite poet Longfellow: *My soul is full of longing for the secrets of the sea, and the heart of the great ocean sends a thrilling pulse through me.*"

"You really have caught the bug, haven't you?" He couldn't help but stare at her. She was a dream he hadn't known he'd wanted. What would a lifetime with her hold?

"I suppose I inherited it from my father. Speaking with my grandmother today made me realize that." Abruptly, she stood. "I should probably turn in."

Caught off-guard by the sudden turn in the evening, he came to his feet. "You're not going to leave me alone in this big house, are you?"

"You're a big boy, James."

"At least indulge me a game of chess and a nightcap. Theo told me you're quite good."

He didn't miss the conflict in her countenance, but she silently agreed. As they moved across the foyer to the parlor, he placed a hand on her back, but she moved away, breaking the contact.

She settled at a table adorned with chess pieces while James poured a dash of port for each of them. In the soft lamplight, Alice's loveliness squeezed his chest. How had it come to this? He was married to a woman who watched him with distrust in her eyes. He knew he could set it right and confess his true intentions — at least, the gist of his intentions in the beginning — but a tendril of fear wrapped like an icy finger around his spine.

Alice would likely tell him to go to hell, and then he would lose her.

But if he bided his time, he could have it all — Menhaden Fishing *and* Alice. And she never need be the wiser. He ignored the twinge of his conscience that seemed to be pressing more and more to be heard.

He brought the drink to her and watched as her slender fingers took it from him. He clinked his glass to hers in a toast. "To the marriage of an Endicott and a Martel. My folks are probably turning in their grave as we speak."

Alice tilted her head to gaze at him. She took a sip of the sweet wine then stood, remaining close to him.

115

Her demeanor was almost rebellious as he looked into her eyes.

"Would your mother approve of me?" she asked softly.

His body reacted to her nearness, as it always did. "I rather think she would. She'd like your gumption."

"I never thought of myself as having that."

"Then you've underestimated yourself, Alice. I'm learning not to do that."

She shook her head. "I wish I could trust you."

James brought a finger to her face, pushed a stray curl away from her cheek, and tucked it behind her ear, noting a barely perceptible shudder resonating from her. "We have time to work on this."

"I'm not so sure about that."

"Why do you say that?"

"Just a feeling."

James sensed the wall she erected between them.

"Did you know that my birthday is less than a fortnight away?" she asked, her tone fractious.

He paused before lying. "No, I didn't."

"I'll be turning twenty-one on Christmas Eve."

His mouth went dry. "Then we should celebrate."

"I imagine that some of us will."

Collecting himself, he sought to smooth over the direction of the conversation. "I'm glad you told me. It would be highly remiss of me to have forgotten such an important day for you."

She made a neutral sound, then said, "Who knows? Maybe I'll come into an inheritance."

"Is that what Daniel told you?"

She narrowed her gaze, her blue eyes flashing like the beam from a lighthouse. "Isn't that what *you* think, James?"

"What exactly are you saying?" he asked, seeking to redirect the glare away from him.

"That your goal in marrying me was to gain *something* and then divorce me."

"I have no intention of ending our marriage." At least that part was true. "I want you, Alice. If we consummate it, I'll honor the union. I make that promise to you."

In an effort to end the discussion, he brought his hands to her cheeks and captured her mouth with his. She wasn't warm and welcoming, but he held his ground, slanting his lips over hers, seeking to incite the hunger he knew lay dormant inside her.

When she yielded, ever so slightly by leaning into him, he wrapped her into his arms as if he held heaven on earth. She pulsed in his blood like the sea that lived in a sailor's veins, a mad desire that could only be appeased one way.

"Alice." He released labored breaths. "Let's go upstairs."

She stilled but he continued to kiss her.

"Don't think," he whispered. "Just feel."

She pulled back, putting far too much distance between them. "No. I can't be swept away by your roguish charm."

He ran his thumb across her lips. "I'll be gentle with you."

"I won't deny that I'm curious about you, and about *this*. But I need time to decide, to be certain."

James rested his forehead to hers. "I won't let you go, Alice."

She brought her gaze to his. "We'll see about that."

As she turned to go, James grasped her hand and tugged her back to him, standing behind her, and nibbled the soft skin along her neck. "If you change your mind, you can come to me at any time."

A slight shiver rippled through her, and, if James was being honest, he was afflicted with a similar shudder.

She lingered, then left without another word or glance back to him.

For several long moments, he remained rooted to where he stood, seeking to quiet the storm that touching his wife had unleashed.

Alice obviously knew of her inheritance. Would she let him take ownership of Menhaden Fishing? Or would she hand it back to Daniel Endicott?

He had never planned to remain married, but now it was clear he needed to hold onto her until Christmas Eve.

Damn. He wanted her for longer than that. Forever, maybe.

He shook his head.

How had it come to this?

20

At breakfast, Alice sat in silence, her stepfather at the head of the table on her right, and James across from her. If three people had the least to say to one another, it was them. Silverware clinked against china as the men ate steak and eggs, while Alice sipped coffee and nibbled on a sweetbread.

"How is Menhaden Fishing, financially?" she asked, looking at Daniel.

James coughed, as if choking on his food, and Daniel glanced up sharply from reading the newspaper.

"Why would that concern you?" Daniel asked.

"I've heard talk," she hedged, "that it's an important asset you own." She looked at her husband. "Do you know anything about the company? It's located in Tiverton."

James stared, neither confirming nor denying the question.

"Such matters aren't for young women to ponder." Daniel waved the maid forward to refill his coffee.

"But Lillie Jenkins does," Alice replied. "Is it wrong of her to be involved in business matters?"

Daniel huffed. "Frankly, yes. She hasn't the capacity to handle it. That's the stone-cold truth."

Alice shifted her gaze to James. "What do you think?"

"It's a challenge for women because they aren't normally raised for such a livelihood, but that doesn't mean they can't learn." James regarded her with a guarded curiosity. "Did you study business at that boarding school of yours?"

"No," Alice replied reluctantly.

"What is it you want to know?" James asked.

"How does the fishing of the menhaden work?"

"Well, most boats employed in the acquisition of pogies are steamers. They capture the fish in great purse-seines—large nets that hang vertically in the water. They're thrown in bulk into the vessel's hold where they stay until transferred to an oil factory, where they're processed."

"How much fish is considered a good season?"

James thought for a moment. "It depends, but about 30,000 barrels would be a very successful run for the year. But that's only a fraction of the total take from all the companies and individual steamers working out on the bay."

"So the real trick is to understand where the pogies are and to get to them first."

James nodded. "To simplify it, yes."

Daniel slapped the newspaper onto the table. "There's nothing simple about any of it." He looked at James. "I wonder how you're able to twiddle your thumbs here in Newport. Who's running *your* fishing company?"

"My brother Frank is quite capable."

An expression of skepticism crossed Daniel's features. "Son, you should've sold Martel Enterprises to me when you had the chance."

"You want to sell your company?" Alice asked James, surprised.

"No." Tension simmered in James' dark gaze. "I don't."

"It can be difficult to keep the bottom line healthy," Daniel said, standing. "There's no shame in walking away from a sinking ship."

"Spoken from a man who sinks ships as a matter of course," James said.

"Well, unlike you, Martel, I have work to do." Daniel glanced at her. "Alice."

She acknowledged her stepfather's departure with a nod.

The change in James' demeanor was difficult to miss. He brooded. Having no patience in wanting to smooth his ruffled feathers, she took her leave of him.

21

Wanting to purchase Christmas gifts for her grandmother and Vera, Alice instructed the carriage driver to take her to the shopping district. Perhaps the diversion would keep her mind off her impending inheritance and the outcome of her marriage.

She debated whether to buy something for her husband since she honestly didn't know how much longer he would fill that role.

Whenever James was near, she felt alive in ways she never had before. What if she simply trusted him? What if she gave him her heart and the keys to Menhaden Fishing as soon as Daniel was forced to hand them over to her? Would James do right by her? Would he return her love?

Plagued with doubt, and knowing she needed to keep him at arm's length until after her birthday, she focused on what she should acquire for the two women.

She told the driver, Stanley, to stop the carriage before an elegant glass shop. Alice entered and perused the selections, seeking two inexpensive vases. It was James' money she spent, and she thought it wise to be frugal.

But soon, she would have her own income. She was about to come into possession of a fishing enterprise.

The thought filled her with excitement as well as anxiety. While she had no idea how to run such a company — although, after quizzing James this morning, it seemed fairly straightforward — the idea buzzed in her ear that she could be independent from both her husband *and* her stepfather, and that filled her with immense satisfaction.

If James left her, she could still live a life on her own.

Buoyed by the possibility, she shifted her attention to the pretty glassware. Choosing two, she had them wrapped and brought out to the carriage.

"Where's your husband?" Alice jumped and spun around at William Evans sudden appearance.

Composing herself, she glared at him, ignoring the frisson of fear that shot through her. "I came out for a bit of shopping. Good day." She turned and attempted to climb into the carriage, not about to wait on the curb until her driver returned.

William grabbed her arm, and she stumbled back.

Terrified, she struggled to get free. William had been like this before she'd run away to Boston, and it was one of the reasons she'd fled.

He twisted her around and pinned her against the carriage, his hands painfully holding her in place. "You're an idiot, Alice."

She refused to look him in the eye, but she couldn't ignore the smell of liquor on his breath.

"I'll have what's mine," he hissed. "You'll see. You can't humiliate me by marrying someone else and get away with it."

Words caught in her throat. She should scream and struggle, because then, surely, some bystander would help, but her limbs were frozen in panic.

"Get your hands off her," a man's voice boomed.

James. She nearly fainted from relief.

William's jaw flexed as he paused, but he released her. She stepped to the side as James faced the seething, drunk man.

"I thought I told you to stay away from my wife."

"I'm beginning to think that you tricked Alice into marrying you," William spat out. "Daniel will end this soon. You have no idea what you've done."

"And you have no idea how much I dislike you." James moved closer.

Fear snaked down Alice's spine. "James, let's just go — please." She reached out to touch his arm, but then pulled it back. Even James' behavior left her unsettled.

Where was her driver?

She glanced around. People had begun to take notice of them.

"Alice was mine," William ground out. "You have no right to her."

Without warning, William punched James in the face, knocking him back. Alice screamed as he swiftly recovered and barreled into William. She stepped aside just as they fell to the ground.

They rolled, James gaining the upper hand, but William struck him in the ribs.

Stunned by how quickly it had all happened, Alice was thankful when several gentlemen interceded, hauling James away from William, who lay on the ground holding his nose as blood poured from it.

James jerked away from the men.

Her middle-aged driver appeared, eyes wide.

"Stanley, we need to leave," she said.

"Yes, ma'am."

"Get in the carriage, James," she demanded.

He didn't respond, his feral gaze locked on William.

Stanley helped her into the buggy. Once inside, she looked at James through the open door where he stood.

"You'll be sorry about this," William yelled, standing. He tried to stop the flow of blood now covering his gray suit and waistcoat.

"As will you," James replied, his rigid frame pulsating with restrained violence.

Alice was on the verge of instructing Stanley to leave James behind when her husband finally regained his senses and swung his eyes to her. What she saw stopped her cold. A savage inhabited his body, putting her in mind of a wolf on the hunt.

He stepped into the carriage and took a seat opposite her, wiping blood from the corner of his mouth with the back of his hand. He banged on the door to signal Stanley to proceed. The carriage pitched forward as the horses were set in motion.

Alice reached into her reticule and pulled a kerchief from it, silently handing it to James. He smeared red blood onto the silky white material, serving as a commemoration of the altercation.

James watched her with a hooded expression. "Don't ever go near him again."

Indignation filled her. "I didn't. He accosted *me*."

"Did you love him?"

Stunned by the sudden change in the conversation, Alice wavered. Love was the furthest thing she'd ever felt for William Evans. "No. I thought we'd already discussed this."

James looked out the window. "Yes, we have." He let out a deep exhale. "I just thought...that maybe you went out today to meet him."

Vexed by his accusation, she fought to keep her anger contained. "I can most assuredly tell you I did not."

He locked his eyes to hers. "My apologies, Alice." The savage relinquished control, and in its place, the James she knew returned. "I just wonder if you divorce me, will you end up married to him?"

"Never."

He laughed, but it was without merriment. "You must think me a brute."

Despite his behavior with William, she knew he was no barbarian. But Vera's words came back to her. *There was talk of retribution from the Martel's...* She had to know. "Do you often resort to violence?"

"No, I don't." He watched her. "I would never hurt you."

Perhaps it was foolish, but she believed him.

She nodded and stared at the clamor of town as the rhythmic swaying of the carriage muffled her thoughts, which was just as well. She was weary of the game of trying to anticipate what the outcome might be. Would her stepfather truly hand over Menhaden Fishing to her? What if he found a way not to honor the agreement?

She wished she could confide in James, hand over all her worries and let him deal with it. She longed to trust him as a wife *should* trust her husband. But what if she did, and he ruined her as Daniel had ruined James' father? Was that his true aim?

She didn't know him, not in any way that warranted such faith.

And yet, her heart ached for him.

She glanced at his profile; his blue-green eyes flashed azure today from beneath brooding dark eyebrows. His strong jawline flexed, and a streak of blood had smeared near his chin. She scooted to the edge of her seat and leaned forward. He watched her as she licked her thumb then rubbed gently on his skin to remove the smudge.

"There was still blood..."

He stilled her hand with his, his skin cool from the chill outside. His gaze transfixed her, filled with an unwavering possession that went straight to her toes. He desired her, and not just her body.

"What are we going to do about this, Alice?"

Raising her face to his, she kissed him, and in one desperate surge, he devoured her mouth.

Alice didn't back down, unleashing all the pent up hunger and desire and curiosity that she'd kept bottled up since the day of their wedding.

Losing herself to the wanton display, her inhibitions obliterated, she reveled in the woodsy scent of his skin, in the lingering taste of coffee in his mouth. He crushed his lips to hers and hauled her atop his lap, pushing her bonnet from her head.

Breathing heavily, Alice ran her fingers into his black tresses, touching him as if her life depended on it, and slanted her lips onto his again. His tongue swept her mouth, and in a delirium, she joined hers with his.

Abruptly the carriage halted, and the sound of Stanley's boots hitting the ground jolted Alice to awareness. She broke the embrace and threw herself back against the opposite bench. She grabbed her bonnet and quickly planted it atop her head and re-tied the ribbon, her hands trembling.

James watched her, his lust undisguised. "Alice."

She shook her head. As soon as Stanley opened the door, she threw herself from the carriage, ran into the house, up the stairs and into her bedroom, then locked the door. Only then did she allow herself to catch her breath. She closed her eyes as she leaned back against the door.

God help me, I love him.

22

Alone in the parlor, James ruminated over his wife, seeking to tamp down the unquenchable desire that she so easily ignited in him.

He burned for Alice, and, if it wasn't so damn maddening, he'd laugh about his predicament.

It didn't help that he'd seen her with William, the man standing close, his hands clutching her as if they shared an intimate secret. The anger he'd felt caught him quite by surprise. All he could think was that Alice was his.

He'd never been possessive or jealous over the handful of women he'd been involved with. He slumped in the leather chair and rubbed a hand down his face. He wanted nothing more than to take his wife into his arms and make love to her so she could understand that their connection wasn't ordinary. She needed to know that

129

this didn't happen every day. No other woman had ever come close to his heart.

But isn't that precisely what he'd wanted to avoid?

He stood and began to pace.

A housemaid appeared. "A letter, sir."

James took it and nodded. She departed, and he unfolded the message. It was from Frank.

James,

How goes it with the snake?

Some news. I've just heard from a reliable source that Menhaden Fishing is about to lose its contracts with the oil factories they use up north. Daniel Endicott has been squeezing them for pricing, and they're fed up.

When we take Menhaden Fishing, we'll have to act quickly to restore those contracts.

Frank

It was suddenly clear why Endicott was interested in Lillie Jenkins. He wanted her oil factories.

In three days Alice would turn twenty-one. Then, James would have his hands on Menhaden Fishing as well as his wife. He'd take her back to Tiverton where he'd make amends and show Alice that they could have a real marriage.

And he would attempt to sign contracts with Lillie directly. That would help everyone involved, while leaving Daniel Endicott out of it.

James shook his head. How did it come down to him having to convince two headstrong females to get the rewards he sought?

* * * *

Later that day, Alice left the Endicott mansion and had Stanley drive her to Vera's dress shop. She had the glass vase—wrapped and adorned with a bow—in hand. She planned to give it to Vera, since she didn't know when she would have a chance to see her before Christmas.

Alice had stayed in her bedroom for much of the day, and James hadn't disturbed her. She didn't know whether she should be happy or concerned. Nevertheless, when she'd finally descended to the first floor she'd learned that he was gone. Daniel was absent as well.

Alice entered the dress shop. Vera's current customer turned around.

"Lillie?"

"Alice, how nice to see you." Lillie smiled warmly and came forward for a hug, dressed in a lavender coat and the hat with the bird's nest Alice had seen her wearing weeks ago at the Tiverton Train Station.

Alice couldn't help but like the woman's genuineness. All the more reason why James would admire her as well.

"Do you know one another?" Vera asked.

"Yes. We've been recently acquainted." Alice handed the gift to Vera. "This is for you. I wanted to drop it off before things became hectic with the holidays."

"Thank you, my sweet." Vera beamed. "You didn't have to do this."

"I know, but I wanted to do something nice for you."

As Vera went to the front of the store to place the gift under a Christmas tree adorned with popcorn garland and red ribbons, Lillie said, "Are you and James still staying with your stepfather?"

"Yes."

Lillie's expression became solemn. "I imagine James doesn't like it and is being difficult."

"A little, I suppose."

Vera returned. "Would you both like some tea while I get Mrs. Jenkins' order wrapped up for her?"

"That would be lovely," Lillie replied.

Alice smiled to hide her uncertainty.

Once they were settled in the parlor where Alice had learned of the fate of the Martels at the hands of Daniel Endicott, a debate began in her mind. She needed a friend. But could she rely on Lillie Jenkins?

"I hope you don't think me impertinent," Alice began, "but why do you spend time with my stepfather?"

Lillie added a dash of cream to her tea then stirred. When she set the spoon on the saucer, the noise filled the silence in the room. Lillie took a sip then deposited the cup back to its resting place.

She was refined and elegant, and quite beautiful, and Alice found herself wishing she was more like this woman.

"Daniel can be very...demanding." Lillie sighed. "I don't want to offend you, Alice, by saying something hurtful about your stepfather."

"There's little you could say that would convince me he's a man of high conviction and flawless intention."

Lillie stared at her, then laughed. Alice smiled, somewhat relieved.

"Please tell me you won't marry him," Alice said. "I saw what it did to my mother. I wouldn't wish the same for you."

Lillie's bearing changed. Gone was the warm-hearted woman from before; in her place was a somber specimen with a shrewd countenance. "I'm not a naive young girl. I think James still believes I am and seeks to protect me, due to his friendship with Stephen, but I'm perfectly capable of running my own life. I miss my husband with all my heart, but I won't lie down and give up on life simply because he's gone. He wouldn't want that. But I also won't be coddled by the men around me. I plan to run Stephen's businesses myself."

"Truly?" Alice asked, intrigued.

"Which brings me back to the naive young girl—you. Alice, I love James. As I told you, he's like a brother to me, but it distresses me to think that he might've taken advantage of you. How is it that you met again?"

Alice faltered. "I'm not sure I should tell you."

"I'm not pressing you. You can share as much or as little as you wish."

Alice took a steadying breath. "I'm a mail-order bride."

Lillie's eyes widened. "Good Lord. I've heard of such things, but I always thought the women were desperate."

An apprehensive laugh escaped Alice. "I suppose we are, but I'd like to think we're women willing to take a risk and embrace the adventure of an entirely new situation."

Lillie abandoned her tea and slumped back against the sofa. "James actually sent for a mail-order bride?"

Alice shook her head. "No. It was his brother, Frank."

Recognition dawned on Lillie's face. "Ah. That makes more sense. Frank has always been a tad impetuous." Lillie's brows knit together. "So why aren't you married to him?"

"When I arrived, Frank was already spoken for. James agreed to take his place."

Lillie shook her head. "This sounds so unlike James. Does he treat you well?"

"Yes, of course." Before Alice could consider the ramifications of baring her soul to the other woman, she plunged ahead. "But we haven't consummated the marriage."

133

"Oh." Lillie became silent.

"At first I thought it was because of me," Alice continued nervously, "but now *I'm* keeping him out of my bedchamber."

"Is there a reason the two of you haven't, well, you know?"

Alice nodded. "I've recently learned some news that seems to put our marriage into a different perspective. On my twenty-first birthday, which is in three days' time, I'm to inherit Menhaden Fishing."

Once again, Lillie was speechless. Then, after the span of several seconds, she began to laugh, rocking back and forth, one arm holding her stomach and the other covering her face. She leaned forward, her chin upon the hand she'd used to hide her mirth. "Alice, I can't emphasize this enough. Do not let these men run your life."

"I'm trying, but I don't have many resources."

Lillie's eyes sparkled. "I can help you with that. I have a lawyer—who can't be swayed by the power of Daniel Endicott, I might add—and I understand the fishing business." She paused. "Do you know the history between James' father and Daniel concerning Menhaden Fishing?"

"Yes, I do."

"James told you?" Lillie asked in surprise.

"No. I learned of it elsewhere."

"Well then. I can tell that you've deduced this might be why James married you. Does he know about the inheritance?"

Alice chewed her lower lip. "I don't know how he could, but he must. I believe he means to divorce me and take it once I receive ownership. I suppose I can't blame him. Menhaden Fishing belonged to his father, after all. He simply wants it back."

"But he used you to get it." Lillie narrowed her eyes. "That's rather backhanded in my book, if you ask me."

"But we're married, and as soon as I inherit—presuming, of course, that my stepfather doesn't have something up his sleeve—James will take over, end our marriage, and be on his merry way."

Lillie reached for Alice's hand. "What is it that you wish from all of this?"

Taken aback by the question, the answer bubbled up from the depths of Alice's soul. "I want a real marriage with James. I can't help it, but I love him. I also want something of my own. I want to run Menhaden Fishing myself, but to be honest, I don't know the first thing of how to go about it."

Lillie retrieved her teacup and sipped thoughtfully, watching Alice with a cool gaze. "In the beginning, I didn't understand business either, but Stephen was patient with me. He taught me much. I can't say whether James would be as patient with you, but if you'll let me, I can help you."

"Why would you do this?"

Lillie grinned. "Bravo. You're wise to be skeptical. Already you're headed in the right direction." She leaned forward. "All right, I *will* expect something in return."

"What would that be?"

"First, that we be friends. Second, that you'll negotiate an exclusive contract with my fish oil factories in Tiverton once you own Menhaden Fishing."

"But James will technically own it."

"Not if I can help it."

23

James was relieved when Alice made an appearance for dinner. He hadn't seen her all day, not since the steamy kiss in the carriage this morning, and anticipation for her company had swirled in his belly since. He'd sought to give her space, and she had apparently taken him up on it. Daniel Endicott was away and had left word that he'd return in the morning. He'd also requested a private meeting with Alice.

"You don't have to see him alone." James spooned the aromatic mushroom soup into his mouth. He'd forgotten to eat a noon-day meal. Thoughts of Alice all but consumed his mind of late. Sitting across from him, she was stunning, and he found it difficult to take his eyes from her.

"I'll be fine," she answered.

"You look exceptionally beautiful this evening." He leaned back as the maid took his empty soup dish and replaced it with a plate filled with pork roast and golden potatoes.

The maid exchanged the dishes before Alice. "Thank you."

He waited until they were alone again before asking, "Where did you go this afternoon?"

She sipped a glass of sherry. "To visit my friend Vera at her dress shop. I wanted to give her a gift that I purchased this morning."

"About this morning..."

Alice cleared her throat. "Let me ask you something."

He stopped slicing his meat and gave her his full attention. "Of course."

"Do you truly think we could have a long marriage? Is that something that you want?"

Guilt gnawed at the edges of James' reasoning. He hadn't been honest with her from the start. Frank had brought her from Boston under an egregious pretense. "There are many things I want, Alice, but we don't always get the things we desire, do we?"

She took a large gulp of her sherry and set it hard upon the table. "No, we don't."

Like a cold splash of water, the reality of the situation hit James. There was no guarantee their marriage would survive. In a few days, he'd have possession of the one thing he'd desired all along— Menhaden Fishing. If Alice couldn't forgive him for absconding with her inheritance, then divorce was still a real possibility. And if he ruined her virtue on top of it, then what kind of man was he?

If Alice hadn't held him off, he'd have damn sure bedded her by now, most assuredly complicating matters. But he had come to care for his stubborn, intelligent wife, and he didn't want to hurt her, at least no more than he could help.

Dinner proved to be a solemn affair, and when Alice excused herself, James let her go.

* * * *

The next morning, Alice took a small breakfast in her room. She'd tossed and turned all night, worrying, and awoken with even less appetite than she'd had sleep.

She drank half a cup of coffee and ate a boiled egg before descending the stairs to her stepfather's study where he sat behind the desk. She closed the door behind her.

"Please sit down." Daniel collected a pile of papers and set them aside. "I'm happy to see you still here at the house, although I'd be happier to see James Martel elsewhere."

Alice sat in the chair facing the desk and didn't respond.

Daniel folded his hands and gave her a stern look. "I really think we should talk about this."

"About what?"

"About this hasty marriage. I did a bit of investigating. All the girls from that factory where you worked became mail-order brides, not just a few of them. Is that what you are, Alice?"

Alice fought to squelch the sting of reprimand in her stepfather's voice. "It doesn't really matter. I'm an adult. I can make my own decisions."

Daniel sighed. "I suppose that's true. But you forget that you're an Endicott."

Anger filled her. "I'm not. I'm a Harrington."

Reclining in his chair, Daniel shook his head. "I've done everything I can for you. I took care of your mother. I've managed what your father left behind. I've given you a good life, Alice. I'm only asking for a little respect in return."

She refused to meet his gaze. He was right, of course, and it weighed on her. Was she simply behaving like a foolish girl? Was she wrong to have thrown away the life that he offered her? But that life entailed being married to William Evans, and she knew in every fiber of her body that she didn't want that.

Now, however, she was wed to James Martel, a man she loved but who might prove to be just as bad for her as Evans. While Evans would surely have battered her spirit, James had the power to break her heart. She wondered if she could ever recover from that.

She raised her eyes to her stepfather. "What is it that you want from me?"

His gaze yielded, revealing what appeared to be weariness. "I would like to protect you. I would like to help you end your marriage to James Martel."

"And what do you offer in exchange?"

He arched an eyebrow. "I see you've acquired a backbone. Perhaps menial labor has changed you for the better. What did you do in that factory?"

"I was a seamstress."

He nodded. "Well, I gather you don't wish to marry William, so you can remain here with me. I'll take care of you."

Alice considered the deal. While she had no desire to live the rest of her days with Daniel Endicott, he did have everything that had once belonged to her father. Didn't she owe it to her family to preserve what was rightfully hers? Was she a coward if she ran away? Was she a coward if she stayed?

"We've no time to waste," her stepfather continued. "Your birthday is in two days. And Christmas the following day. We can end this marriage tomorrow before everyone goes on holiday. I know someone in the court system who can expedite this."

Unable to find the words, Alice silently agreed.

24

"Endicott is only chasing you because he wants those contracts." James hadn't meant to raise his voice to Lillie, but her reluctance to acknowledge her vulnerable position with the man annoyed him.

Lillie Jenkins took a sip of tea and gave a slight shake of her head. "It's not like you, James, to make a scene." She glanced around at the restaurant they occupied. Gaiety filled the room; conversation from the patrons at crowded tables swirled in the air and waiters hurriedly saw to their customers. The holiday spirit was in full swing. Garland decorated the walls of the upscale establishment, and a lavish Christmas tree sat in one corner. "You look a bit peaked. Is marriage not agreeing with you?"

"I'm fine. Alice is fine."

Lillie gave a pacifying smile. "You know how much Stephen meant to me. You know how much we loved each other." Her voice broke and she took another sip of tea. "You deserve to have that kind of love, James. And so does Alice."

"What are you saying?"

"I'm saying that your anger about what happened to your father has caused you to take a path that isn't a good one."

James stared at his cup. Lillie had pricked the conscience he did battle with more and more with each passing day.

"As for this business with Endicott," Lillie continued, "I'm well aware of what is going on. I'm not as helpless as you think. While I've appreciated your concern since Stephen passed, along with your efforts to help me, I plan to run his businesses myself."

James raised his eyes to hers. She'd been telling him this all along, but he hadn't believed her. Comprehension finally dawned as he saw the conviction in her expression.

"And for what it's worth," Lillie added, "I suspect I won't be negotiating with Daniel Endicott for much longer."

"Has he mentioned matrimony?"

Lillie's face took on a serene expression. "Arranged marriages aren't my style, so have no fear. But you're no stranger to such a situation, are you?"

James gave a mirthless laugh. "You have a knack for uncovering the truth wherever you go, don't you?"

"I pay attention where I can. It was a trait Stephen both admired and grumbled about. I like Alice. She's a bit unsure of herself, but in time, she'll find her footing. She just needs guidance. She doesn't deserve to be tossed aside."

"I would never toss her aside."

Lillie watched him with a skeptical expression.

"It's complicated, Lillie." He ran a hand through his hair. Is this why she'd requested this meeting? To lecture him about his marriage?

"It doesn't need to be. Do you even care for her?"

His throat closed and his chest tightened as the truth pounded in his skull. "Of course I do."

Lillie stood. "Then remember that."

James came to his feet.

"I'm sure I'll see you again before this is all over." She grasped his arm and stretched upward to kiss his cheek. "I do love you, James. Please remember that as well in the coming days."

And on that cryptic remark, she left the restaurant.

* * * *

Like a rudderless ship, Alice walked down to Newport Harbor with no clear destination or purpose. She passed sailmaker shops and sail-drying lofts, her boots clicking on the brick walkways. Bundled into her coat, she still felt chilled. The emptiness in her heart left no warmth in its wake.

She had agreed to end her marriage. Daniel had already sent a messenger to begin the process. Was it the right thing to do?

Despite whatever brief moments of passion had ignited between her and James, she could never be entirely certain that he wouldn't claim her innocence alongside her inheritance, then leave her emptyhanded, her heart bleeding in the wake.

She needed to be smart about this.

Leaving the safety of the road, she took wooden stairs to Bowen's Wharf and the granite quays that were surrounded by tethered boats. Newport Harbor was considered one of the best on the New England coast, with a natural protection that inhibited freezing during the winter months.

The giant ships beckoned Alice forward, the masts reaching to the gray skies, the endless array of ropes covering the deck like a spider's web. Men milled about, but not many. She suspected most had come home to spend Christmas with their families.

Another wave of despair washed over her. She missed her mother, the longing deep and sharp.

She came to the end of a dock and paused. Beyond was Narragansett Bay and the Atlantic Ocean. She thought of the whales her father had sometimes described to her, giant leviathans that would rise from the depths and glide past his big ship, dwarfing it. At times, he'd said they were violent and wild, and other times languid and serene.

"What would happen if I jumped on the back of one, Papa?" she'd asked him.

"You'd sail to the ends of the earth."

"What would I find?"

"I don't know. When you return you can tell me."

A sad smile tugged at her mouth as she recalled the memory.

Would she own Menhaden Fishing in two days' time? Did she have what it took to run a company and make it successful? And if, by chance, she did triumph, would she one day have enough money to buy her own ship and sail to the horizon, to find what lay out there, to finally tell her Papa?

So many unknowns. She supposed this is what it meant to mature from a child to an adult.

"You shouldn't stand down here, miss."

Alice spun around. A disheveled man approached in tattered clothing. His odor assaulted her, and she coughed to rid the smell from her nose.

"I'm sorry," she replied. "I didn't realize this was private property."

The man kept lumbering toward her, white puffs of cold air spewing from his mouth from his exertions. "It ain't safe."

Alice stepped back, but she had nowhere to go. The edge of the dock dropped directly into the water. And he wasn't slowing down!

She tried to duck away and angle around him, but he pushed her with surprising strength. Screaming, she fell from the platform, dropping into the icy water, the impact knocking the breath from her.

Struggling to the surface, she screamed and gasped as the frigid water slapped her face. The heavy wool coat that covered her gown and layers of petticoats kept the icy fluid from reaching skin, but then the water-soaked garments began to drag her under. She flailed desperately to keep her head afloat. Surely the crazy man who had pushed her would get help.

She yanked her gloves from her hands and worked at the buttons on her coat, finally freeing enough to peel it from her. She didn't sink as much, but now the ocean began to saturate her clothing right down to her skin.

With chattering teeth, she continued to yell for help, but no one came.

She searched for a ladder — anything — that would get her out of the water.

Slowly she began to swim toward a nearby ship, where rope webbing hugged the hull. She could cling to it until aid arrived. Surely someone had seen what happened to her.

Her sluggish limbs became more useless as the minutes ticked by. Concentrating on her movements, she struggled to get her body to obey the commands from her brain.

The webbing was still too far away, and she could no longer feel her legs. She fought to move her limbs the way they ought to, but she had no idea if they obeyed.

Her forward motion stopped.

No.

She wasn't near anything.

Her arms were like heavy trunks, moving too slowly to keep her afloat.

She gasped her last breath of air then slipped below the surface.

25

James arrived at the hospital in a panic.

He rushed to a woman sitting at a desk. "My wife is here — Alice Martel."

The woman scanned a paper on a clipboard. When she didn't respond immediately, James added, "Alice Endicott."

"Oh yes, here she is. She's in room 211, on the second floor." She pointed down the austere hallway. "Take the stairs, then make a right."

He rushed to the second floor, passing nurses in long white aprons. Locating the room, he entered. Alice lay in a bed, her head slightly elevated and her eyes closed. Her blonde hair spilled around her pillow in disarray, and her ashen pallor caused his heart to skip a beat.

A nurse entered from behind. "Pardon me, sir. May I help you?"

James stepped aside and took a deep breath. "Yes. This is my wife. How is she?"

"She's doing better. It took a while to warm her up." The woman approached Alice and tucked a blanket beneath his wife's chin.

James came to her bedside. "What happened?"

"The report says that she fell into the harbor. A fisherman found her, which likely saved her life."

Anger surged through James. "How in the hell did she fall into the water?" He glanced up and saw the shock on the woman's face. "My apologies."

The young nurse gave a curt nod. "I understand." She paused. "The fisherman reported that a vagrant assaulted her, and she was pushed."

Shocked, James shifted his attention back to his wife. "Was the man found?"

"Unfortunately, no. You can stay as long as you wish. It would do well for her to have someone near who loves her." She gave a sympathetic smile and left them alone.

James retrieved a wooden chair from the corner of the room and set it beside the bed. He laid a hand on Alice, buried beneath a pile of blankets. Trying to steady himself as his heart pounded relentlessly, he gave silent thanks to God that she lived.

When the letter had arrived, addressed to Daniel Endicott, informing him that Alice was in the hospital, James hadn't waited for the man to gather himself. He'd foregone a carriage and run the several blocks to the hospital directly, his mind considering every possible outcome.

One thing had become clear. He was desperate not to lose Alice. Everything else had fallen to the wayside.

The door to Alice's room opened, and James knew it was Daniel.

"How is she?" Endicott asked.

James kept his focus on Alice. "She's alive."

Daniel came to the opposite side of the bed, his usual arrogant demeanor gone, the jowls under his cheeks more prominent than usual. "What on earth happened to her?"

"She was pushed into the harbor." James didn't try to hide the seething anger in his voice.

"By whom?" Daniel asked, clearly stunned.

James watched the elder man closely. "The report states it was a vagrant, but such men are easily persuaded with the right incentive."

Daniel clamped his mouth shut and narrowed his eyes. "Are you insinuating that I'm responsible for this?"

"Tomorrow is Alice's birthday, and she'll inherit Menhaden Fishing."

"How do you know that?"

James stood. "Perhaps trusting William Evans was your downfall."

Daniel swore under his breath.

"It would be a lot easier if you got rid of her," James continued.

"You need to stop right there, young man. I would never harm Alice."

"But you would force her to marry a man she doesn't love?"

Daniel's nostrils flared as he inhaled and exhaled. "I was trying to do what was best for her. And yes, I want to keep Menhaden Fishing."

"It's not your company."

Daniel sighed. "Yes, it is. I'm sorry about your father, but business is business. He was man enough to understand that. You should be too." He paused. "That's it, isn't it? That's why you married Alice—to get your father's company back. And you dare to lecture me about right and wrong."

James clenched his jaw so hard he flinched from the pain. "Perhaps, in the beginning, that was my intention. You hurt my family, so I returned the favor."

Alice moved, and when James glanced down at her, he saw her eyes wide open. He knew, without a doubt, that she'd heard the last words from his mouth.

Her gray face and colorless lips squeezed his chest, but her words effectively sucked the life from him. "I want a divorce."

26

Fatigue overwhelmed Alice, and now despair. When she awoke to hear James' words—*you hurt my family, so I returned the favor*—it was a blow she had anticipated, but nevertheless, the world spun away from her with a stunning finality. Her heart was now well and truly broken.

"You don't mean this."

She refused to acknowledge the edge in his voice. "I don't want to do this anymore, James," she whispered. "I'm sorry for what happened to your family, but I'm done being used by you." She closed her eyes to shut him out.

"Alice, you don't understand." His voice broke. "I love you."

She knew they were empty words. Opening her eyes, she accused, "How dare you say that. I just want you to go."

"This is too much for her, James," Daniel cut in. "You need to let her rest."

Distress played across James' handsome face. He appeared haggard and half-dressed with his shirt unbuttoned near the neckline and no tie. Was that remorse in his eyes? A part of her wanted to believe it, but still, it wasn't enough.

"Fine, I'll go," James conceded. "But this isn't over. You're my wife, Alice. I won't let you go that easily."

Alice didn't have the strength to respond.

Once James left the room, tears streamed down her face.

"It'll be fine," Daniel said, gently patting her shoulder. "I'll take care of everything."

* * * *

Alice awoke in the afternoon to find her grandmother sitting beside her.

Edith smiled. "I hope you don't mind that I came."

"No." Alice all but croaked, her throat parched and scratchy. "How long have you been here?"

"A few hours. I saw Daniel Endicott and told him I would stay with you so he could leave. How are you feeling?"

"Very tired."

"Do you remember what happened?"

Alice tried to recall the incidents of the previous day, but her mind felt shrouded in fog. "Did I die?"

Her grandmother faltered. "The nurse said that you may have been gone for a short time."

Alice stared up at the ceiling, trying to remember when the freezing ocean had swallowed her up. "How did I get pulled from the water?"

"A fisherman saw you. Thank the good Lord." Edith paused. "I spoke with Daniel, and he told me of your circumstances, about you ending your marriage. I'm sorry I was never able to meet your husband. I

151

wanted to offer you a place in my home, at least for now. I could look out for you. I realize your stepfather has staff that could do that for you, but I'm your family and I'd like to help."

The offer warmed a tiny portion of Alice's heart, and she was grateful for the gesture. She pulled her arm from beneath the covers and grasped her grandmother's hand. "Thank you. I think I would like that."

Edith handed her a book. "I wanted to give you this. It belonged to Gavin and was a favorite of his. I thought you might like to have it."

Alice gazed at a well-worn copy of poetry by Henry Wadsworth Longfellow. Moved by the gift, Alice said softly, "He was Papa's favorite."

"Yes. I'm not sure how I ended up with it, but after your visit, I found a trunk filled with Gavin's things and this was inside."

Alice opened the book to an earmarked page.

It is foolish to pretend that one is fully recovered from a disappointed passion. Such wounds always leave a scar.

It was as if her father was in the room with her, offering her support and a shoulder to cry upon.

Her soul whispered her heartbreak...*James*...

* * * *

That evening, Alice awoke from yet another long slumber. She wished she could sleep forever. At least, then, she didn't have to experience the aching emptiness in her heart over James' betrayal.

She pushed herself upright and reached for a glass of water on the nightstand when someone knocked at the door. Lillie Jenkins appeared.

"Are you taking visitors?" she asked.

Alice touched her hair self-consciously. "Of course, but I must look a fright."

Lillie waved her off, came forward and hugged her.

Emotion overtook Alice, and she clung to the woman, who eased herself to sit on the edge of the bed.

"Oh, now, now," Lillie crooned. "You're safe."

Embarrassed by her outburst, Alice released Lillie and ducked her head, but she couldn't stifle the tears that welled in her eyes.

Lillie pulled a handkerchief from her reticule and dabbed it to the corner of Alice's eye. "It's a miracle that you survived, but I knew that you were strong. *You* just don't know it yet."

"Lillie, it's all a mess. James admitted that he married me to hurt my stepfather, that he meant to take my inheritance from me."

Lillie became serious. "Did he now?" she murmured.

"Daniel wants me to divorce him, and I agreed. I told James, but he said he loves me. And now I'm so confused." The sobs poured forth, and she couldn't rein them in. Lillie handed her the kerchief. "Daniel is sending someone here tonight with the papers."

Lillie placed a palm against Alice's cheek. "Oh my dear, it will be fine. Men can be so obtuse and narrow-minded when they think they know the right plan to follow." Lillie wiped at a stray tear with her thumb and smiled. "Do you love him, Alice?"

"With all my heart."

"Then don't give up so easily."

"But I'm an Endicott, if only by marriage, but one nonetheless. I understand that it would be difficult for James to spend his life tied to a family he despises."

"That's for James to decide."

Alice met Lillie's stern gaze. She was right. It was time for Alice to determine what kind of life she would lead. And she wanted it with James.

"Have you and James consummated your marriage yet?" Lillie asked.

Alice shook her head.

"Good." Lillie grinned. "James doesn't deserve the easy road with you. But more importantly, my lawyer can use that loophole to help you with the ownership of Menhaden Fishing. Listen to me. Don't sign those papers that Daniel sends over just yet. Isn't your birthday tomorrow?"

"Yes."

"I think a party is in order. Will you let me plan it?"

Alice took a deep breath and nodded, an upwelling of hope suffusing her body clear down to her toes.

27

In his room at the Ocean House Hotel, James dressed in his finest suit. He had every intention of heading to Daniel Endicott's estate once this dinner with Lillie was finished. She'd insisted that he meet her in the dining room of the hotel. He was really of no mind for small talk, with Alice forever holding court in his thoughts.

He'd botched it up well with her. He buttoned his shirt, impatience clamoring at him.

'I want a divorce.'

Those were the very words he'd planned to say to her when this was all said and done, but she'd beaten him to it. When he thought he'd lost her he knew he'd been blind to the true gift handed to him when Frank brought her to Tiverton from Boston.

He loved her, and now he'd lost her.

Shrugging into his jacket, he really couldn't blame her.

He should've told her the truth from the start, but if he had it was likely she wouldn't have stayed with him. He would never have had the chance to come to know her, to appreciate her sweet innocence and surprising fortitude.

He settled a burgundy ascot tie below his chin.

The divorce papers arrived last night, but he refused to sign them.

With his attire in order, he paused to scan the room. It was the same one he'd shared with Alice a few weeks ago, before she decided to move back in with her stepfather. Alice had been willing to accept her role as his wife, but he'd kept her at bay, like a fool. If he could turn back time, he'd lock himself up in this room with her and make love to his wife until the New Year rang in. Damn him for letting that opportunity slip through his fingers.

Alice was the best that life had to offer. With a heavy heart, James acknowledged he could never do better. She was an Endicott, that was true, but deep down she was simply herself. And the woman he loved with all his heart.

* * * *

James followed the waiter to a room at the rear of the hotel restaurant. It was quiet on this Christmas Eve, with only a handful of guests enjoying a meal. He passed a large tree festively adorned with red ribbons, pinecones, and porcelain dolls. James' hand went to his jacket pocket, ascertaining the gift for Alice was still there. One way or another, he meant to give it to her this evening—a combined birthday and Christmas gift.

The waiter halted and stepped aside, indicating James to enter. James nodded to the man and, expecting to see Lillie, he froze when his gaze locked on Alice.

She wore an ocean blue gown, simple in construction, with her hair pinned and adorned with tiny white flowers. He'd always liked her this way — natural and basic. She was a beautiful girl and would grow to be an exquisite woman; she didn't require any fancy accoutrements. Her azure eyes held him spellbound, and he couldn't find any words.

"James, I'm so glad you could come," Lillie said as she approached him.

A swift glance around the room showed the presence of Daniel Endicott and two elderly women he didn't recognize, along with a man he knew to be Lillie's attorney.

"We're celebrating Alice's twenty-first birthday," Lillie continued, looping her arm around his. "Please come in and have a seat. We've been waiting for you."

Still stunned by Alice's willingness to share company with him, he looked at Lillie, the fog of confusion slowly lifting. "What's going on?"

Dressed in a green and red gown, Lillie guided him to a seat at the round table. "Everyone who is important to Alice is in this room. You're acquainted with Daniel, of course."

Endicott scowled in his direction.

"This is Vera McAdams, a dear family friend," Lillie continued.

James took the delicate hand of the older woman and nodded.

Lillie turned to the remaining guest. "And this is Edith Harrington, Alice's grandmother."

"I'm pleased to meet you, ma'am," he said. "I'm sorry it couldn't have been sooner."

The woman's cool response made him think he had one foot out the door.

"Everyone, please have a seat," Lillie said.

Alice came to sit beside him, and James quickly pulled her chair for her.

He tugged at his collar in an attempt to cool the sweat forming at the base of his neck. Was this to be some final farewell? A giant send-off before Alice cut him loose permanently?

He took his seat and leaned toward her. "You look beautiful tonight. And a happy birthday to you."

"Thank you." She flashed him a look of apprehension and longing.

He wished they were alone so he could say more.

"You look well, Alice," Daniel said from across the table, "but you didn't respond to my inquiry. I must demand to know why you haven't signed those papers." His eyes darted from Alice to James. "Either of you."

James held his breath. Alice hadn't signed the divorce papers? Dare he hope?

"All in good time, Daniel," Lillie interceded.

James turned to Alice. "Aren't you at the Endicott mansion?"

"No," Alice answered. "My grandmother has been gracious enough to let me stay with her."

"It's no trouble," Edith said. "You can live with me as long as you like."

The news was both a boon and a concern. James was happy that Alice had finally left Daniel's home, but he didn't like the implication that she planned to remain at her grandmother's house for an extended time.

Lillie took a seat beside James and indicated the man to her left. "This is Henry Tavish. He's my lawyer."

James eyed the man with suspicion. "Yes, I know."

Two waiters entered and served port to each guest; when they waited upon James, he quietly asked for a bourbon.

As the drink was delivered, Lillie arched a brow. "Fortification already?"

James savored the smooth liquor as it slid down his throat, immediately loosening tension in his limbs. "What the devil are you up to?" he asked under his breath.

Lillie planted a beatific smile on her lips and turned to her attorney.

Across the table, Daniel watched James with irritation smoldering in his gaze. James supposed the man thought James had something up his sleeve. He had to wonder the same about Daniel.

James downed the remaining liquid in his glass and signaled the waiter for another. He glanced at Alice, who watched him.

"Aren't you having a good time?" she asked.

The alcohol relaxed his tongue. "The last time we spoke, you demanded a divorce. I'm just a little confused as to why I'm here."

Alice shifted her attention to the bowl of soup placed before her. "Lillie thought you would like to be in attendance."

James watched his wife, and his heart twisted. "What I'd really like is to be alone with you."

Her eyes locked with his. The presence of the others fell away, and a connection—raw and wild and authentic—flared between them. He sank into her blue eyes, their depths smoldering with what he hoped was a need as fierce as his own. The creamy hue of her skin emphasized the lushness of her lips. After her near-drowning in the harbor, his heart had all but stopped at the ashen pallor of her skin.

His gaze dropped to her mouth, and he wished to God that he could kiss her.

"Mr. Martel," Vera McAdams inquired, "I understand you run a successful fishing business in Tiverton."

159

James reluctantly dragged his focus away from Alice. "I do well enough, thank you. How is it that you know Alice?"

"I run a dress shop. Alice and her mother were kind enough to support me when I started my business after my husband passed."

"It must run in the family," James replied. "Several years ago Alice's father, Gavin Harrington, offered to assist my father when his business was struggling." He flicked a glance to Daniel. "But some men don't believe in being honorable."

"Yes, I know the story," Mrs. McAdams added quickly.

"You would equate honor with bad business decisions," Daniel said, sitting back to let the waiter clear the soup and place a clean plate before him.

"Sometimes *honor* is more important in the scheme of the world," James said, his temper rising swiftly.

"Now gentlemen," Lillie chimed in, "we're here to celebrate dear Alice's birthday. Let's keep it civil."

The waiters brought a platter of roast beef and mashed potatoes, thick gravy, a dish of fresh corn in melted butter, and a steaming bowl of baked apples. James consumed the meal, all the while aware of Alice beside him as she chatted quietly with Mrs. McAdams.

Once dinner was complete and the table cleared, Lillie stood. "And now it's time to celebrate Alice's birthday on this festive Christmas Eve." She nodded and a waiter signaled for another to enter. A large two-tiered cake covered in ivory frosting and red roses was placed on the table. Everyone stood and clapped.

Alice's face turned crimson. "Thank you, everyone. I know that circumstances haven't always been the best, so I appreciate that you all could be here."

"It's our pleasure," Vera replied.

"Yes, Alice, I'm so happy for you," Edith Harrington said.

Daniel gave a slight nod of acknowledgement. "Happy birthday, Alice."

James raised his glass of port. "To Alice." Everyone did the same. He had many more words he wanted to say, but held back.

A round of, "Here, here," was said.

"Please sit," Lillie instructed. The waiter took the cake to a side table, cut several slices, and distributed the dessert plates to Alice and her guests.

"Now that we're nearing the end of this lovely dinner," Lillie continued, "it's time for Alice's gifts. I hope you all won't mind if I go first. Alice's mother bequeathed to her an exciting business venture to be acquired on her twenty-first birthday — Alice has inherited ownership of Menhaden Fishing, located in Tiverton."

James frowned. Why was Lillie involved with this?

"What are you talking about?" Daniel demanded.

"It's no use denying it or keeping it a secret," Lillie chided. "Mr. Tavish here has all the particulars."

"He's got nothing," Daniel argued.

"On the contrary, Mr. Endicott," Henry Tavish rebutted, retrieving a stack of papers from his leather briefcase. "Hazel Harrington Endicott filed the paperwork, which is signed by you, with a city clerk. I'll admit, it took some searching to locate it, but it's valid. You must uphold the terms of the agreement or be in breach of contract." Tavish hurriedly placed spectacles on his nose and scanned the document. "Yes, it's all right here. Miss Endicott is now the owner of Menhaden Fishing."

Daniel stood, his face bulging in anger. "How dare you meddle in my family's business."

161

James bolted to his feet. "You can direct any complaints you have to *me*. I'm still her husband, and as such, I own the fishery now."

"The day's not over yet," Daniel spat out. "You *will* sign those divorce papers. It's what Alice wanted, and as you believe yourself to be so honorable, such a man would abide by the lady's wishes."

"I must interrupt." Lillie's calm voice belied the order beneath it. "Please sit down, gentlemen."

Reluctantly James took his chair. Alice, Vera and Edith sat rigid and quiet as if corseted by the heavy tension in the room.

Daniel didn't hide a sneer as he finally resumed his seat.

"Actually, Menhaden Fishing *doesn't* belong to you, James," Lillie said.

Surprised, he glanced up at her.

"Forgive my bluntness, but your marriage has remained unconsummated, and as such, the union can't be considered fully legal. Therefore, Alice can take possession of her inheritance directly. Mr. Tavish has prepared the proper documentation on her behalf."

Tavish's head bobbed in agreement, blushing from Lillie's bold statement.

Stunned, James swung his gaze to his wife. Alice met his eyes, no sign of meekness or uncertainty present. She'd managed to take Menhaden Fishing from both him and Daniel. While he couldn't deny the sting from her subterfuge, he couldn't help but admire her initiative. The woman had gumption, just as he'd suspected all along.

A smile graced his lips. "Well played, Alice."

28

Buoyed by the look of admiration in James' eyes, Alice steadied herself. Daniel's outburst had unnerved her, despite the fact she'd expected it.

She fortified herself and shifted her attention to her stepfather. "I don't wish to be divorced. I never did. I understand that James married me to satisfy a vendetta against you and to reclaim what he believed belonged to him." She felt all the eyes at the table on her, but kept her focus. She turned to James. "I'll stay in the marriage, but only if you agree to my terms."

She hoped she didn't misread the look of relief on his face.

"And what would those be?"

"That *I* will own Menhaden Fishing for the length of our marriage, however long that might be. While I may seek your help in business decisions, my main partner will be Lillie Jenkins."

James raised an eyebrow and threw a look in Lillie's direction, not one filled with anger but rather grudging admiration.

"I'm perfectly happy settling in Tiverton and not Newport," she continued, "but I would like you to stop living in the servant's quarters."

"Done."

Taken aback by his swift response, Alice didn't know what to say.

"Oh for God sakes!" Daniel stood and threw his napkin onto the table. "You women can't manage these businesses. You have no idea what you're doing. You'll run it all into the ground. Lillie, marry me, and I can take all this worry away from you. And Alice, you're a young, ignorant girl. Divorce this clodhopper before he makes you any more miserable, and I'll take care of you. I always said I would."

"While I appreciate your offer, Daniel," Lillie said, "I'm not interested in marrying again. I'm prepared to take my chances running Stephen's interests. And you've greatly underestimated Alice. What you call ignorance is simply youth. She's smart, and I can help her."

Daniel shook his head. "You can help yourself. You're taking advantage of her as readily as this man who married her under false pretense."

Alice stood, fueled by outrage. "You took everything that my father had built, but it was never yours to take. My mother married you because she was afraid she'd lose everything, but she managed to preserve this for me, and I won't let her down. Or my father. Lillie Jenkins helped me when I had no one else, and for that, I'll always be grateful. I'm an adult now, Daniel. I no longer require your help."

He shook his head. "You're making a terrible mistake, but let's be clear. When this all falls to pieces, don't come to me begging for help. You can have that damn Menhaden Fishing. I'm finished with this." And with that, he left the room.

Mr. Tavish chased after him. "If you'll just sign a few papers, sir."

"Don't worry," Lillie said. "Tavish'll get everything in order. He may seem a little jittery, but he's quite good at what he does."

Still reeling from her outburst, Alice could hardly believe that it was over. She looked to Vera beside her, a delighted glow on the woman's face. "You've the look of your father right now."

Edith came around the table and hugged Alice. "She's right. I'm so proud of you, Alice. I hope you'll always let me be here for you." Her eyes shifted to where James stood behind her. "And your husband."

"You both will always be welcome in our home," James said, placing a hand at Alice's back. "And I promise to bring Alice to Newport as often as she wishes."

As her worry slowly dissipated, Alice leaned into her husband, a small bubble of happiness starting to grow in her chest. He'd agreed to her demands. He'd let go of Menhaden Fishing. She felt for the first time that he was willing to make a real marriage, not one based on what he could gain from her.

As James guided Alice into the main dining room, Lillie stepped forward and embraced her. "I'm happy for you both." She gave James a peck on the cheek.

"I had no idea you felt so strongly about pursuing Stephen's businesses," James said to her.

"Sometimes circumstances force you beyond yourself," Lillie replied. "Alice understands."

A flutter of nerves took flight in Alice's abdomen. She was about to embark into uncharted waters, and not just with a new company to run. She anticipated that tonight would be, at long last, her true wedding night.

"Thank you, Lillie," Alice said sincerely. "You've been a genuine friend."

Lillie smiled. "I'll secure carriages for Vera and Edith, and I'll have Tavish wait for you both in the lobby. I think it's best to have everything signed and sealed before you both enjoy your first Christmas as a married couple. Oh, one other thing. Local authorities have determined that William Evans was responsible for bribing that vagrant to push Alice into the harbor. He's been arrested, so he shouldn't bother you anymore." She left them.

"It's a good thing he's in jail," James muttered.

"Yes. I'd hate for you two to get in a scuffle again." Alice glanced to James and saw a glint in his gaze that stole her breath and set her heart to pounding.

"I only get into scuffles for you." He leaned down and tenderly kissed her. She closed her eyes and delighted in the feel of his mouth upon hers, not even caring that they were in public.

Remaining close, his voice low so that no one else could hear, he said, "I have to admit that I didn't have high hopes for this outcome, but I'm eternally grateful that you've given me a second chance. I'll spend the rest of my life making certain you don't regret it. I'm sorry I lied to you. I love you, Alice."

Alice's heart swelled, and she couldn't help herself—she threw her arms around him and buried her face into his neck. "I love you too, James. I believe that I always did, maybe as far back as our first meeting at the train station."

He wrapped her into his arms. "Am I really that irresistible?"

"Yes," she replied, her thoughts scattered. "You said that one day, I'd beg you to come to my bed," she whispered. "Well, this is me begging."

"We best get upstairs before you make a spectacle of the both of us."

She nodded, standing back, feeling slightly embarrassed.

With his lips at her ear, he said, "But once we're behind closed doors, Mrs. Martel, you can behave any way you like."

A shiver rippled through her.

Alice couldn't wait to get her husband all to herself.

29

When Alice awoke, James already had breakfast waiting at the oval sitting table before the window, a blustery wind blowing outside. The gray skies, however, couldn't dampen her happiness.

"Good morning." He came to her.

His shirt hung loose, and his hair was still mussed; Alice thought he'd never looked more handsome. Wearing nothing but her chemise, she sat upright, a blaze in the fireplace warming her. But then, so did the man in the room.

He sat on the edge of the bed. "Did you sleep well?"

"Yes." She smiled, remembering the loving and passionate embrace of her husband throughout the night.

"I'm glad. But before I let you eat something, I wanted to give you this." He presented a velvet box upon his large palm. "It is Christmas morning, after all."

"Oh James, I don't have anything for you."

"On the contrary. You've given me the best present I could ask for — you."

He kissed her then handed the gift to her. She opened the box — inside lay a round locket. Carefully inscribed on the top was a quotation from Henry Wadsworth Longfellow.

The dawn is not distant, nor is the night starless; love is eternal.

Tears welled in her eyes. "You remembered that he's my favorite poet," she whispered.

He swiped the stray tears from her cheeks. "I recall all the things that are special about you. I thought maybe you could put a photo of your mother and father inside."

She sniffled and laughed. "Or maybe pictures of our children."

"Or that," he agreed.

"Thank you, James." She became serious. "You're not upset about Menhaden Fishing?"

He watched her. "No. I suppose I was so single-minded in my goal to get it back that I didn't consider others. It'll be in a good hands with you." He grinned. "I think."

She pushed at him in mock derision.

"God help me," he continued, laughing, "I'm going to have to go head to head with you *and* Lillie."

"Perhaps we can work something out since I believe our fleet is larger than yours."

He pushed her back onto the bed. "Is there a way I might garner favor with the new owner."

"It might be possible to work out some type of exchange."

James nuzzled her neck and any further conversation was impossible.

* * * *

December 25, 1890

My Dear Leora,

I'm writing to you on Christmas Day, and it's a most wonderful holiday for me. I can only hope the same is true for you and that you've found happiness with your pastor. I'm happy to report that my marriage to James Martel, Frank's brother, has taken a turn for the better. While it began under a false pretense, and there was much concern as to his motives, I now rest assured in his high regard and love. I was forced to engage with my stepfather despite my every effort in believing that I wouldn't have to, but you'll be pleased to know that I've inherited a fishing company, thanks to the foresight of my mother. I come to my marriage an equal partner, and I can continue the legacy of not only my father, but James' as well.

I miss you and the other girls dearly, and I pray that each of you has found joy and prosperity in your new situations.

Yours Affectionately,
Alice

Epilogue

May 1891

Alice waited eagerly as the Old Colony train pulled into the Tiverton station. As passengers disembarked, she stood on her tiptoes.

"You said she looks like you," James said, standing beside her. "That should make her easy to spot."

Alice laughed. "I hope they weren't delayed."

At that moment, Beth Mitchell Montgomery exited a passenger car, a gentleman behind her.

Alice grabbed James' hand and dragged him along as she pushed forward through the crowd.

Beth grinned upon noticing her and ran the last few steps, then embraced her.

"I'm so thrilled you've come," Alice said, facing her friend once again.

Beth took hold of a tall, dark-haired man's arm. "I want you to meet my husband, George Montgomery."

"It's a pleasure." Alice shook his hand. "And this is my husband, James Martel."

With greetings exchanged, James ushered all of them into a waiting carriage.

Settled across from Beth, Alice couldn't contain her curiosity. "Tell me about the children. How are they?" Beth had written to her of becoming a stepmother to two girls.

"Harriet, who goes by Harry, is six now and is a bundle of energy. She's so curious about everything and loves to climb trees. Genevieve — we call her Genny — is eight and is much more serious. She's always got her nose in a book."

"Sounds like Alice," James remarked. His hand clasped hers.

"Yes," Beth replied, "I remember Alice always had a book of poetry by Longfellow tucked into her skirt pocket when we worked at the factory."

"You had time to read?" George asked. "I heard you ladies were worked to the bone."

"We were," Alice said. "But I'd read snippets on the short breaks. Where are Harry and Genny now?"

Beth smiled at her husband. "We have a lovely housekeeper in Lawrence named Mandy, who is watching them."

They arrived at the Martel home, and Alice welcomed Beth into the parlor while their husbands dispatched the luggage.

Alice shed her bonnet, and Beth did the same. "I'll just make some tea, and we can visit."

"Alice, good grief. You're not to wait on me. Show me where the kitchen is."

Beth followed her down the hallway. Alice put a kettle of water onto the stove and stoked the fire while Beth retrieved teacups, sugar and cream.

"Let's sit while we wait for the water to boil," Alice said. "I'm so glad you've come to visit. Tell me about your Mr. Montgomery."

"It didn't begin as a love match, but I'm happy to say it is now."

"I'm so relieved."

"How are you and James?" Beth asked.

"Well, I have news I've not yet told anyone." Alice couldn't keep the grin from her face. "We're to have a baby."

"Oh Alice, that's wonderful." Beth reached across the small wooden table and squeezed her hand. "I'm hoping soon to have such news as well. Is it really true that you run a fishing company?"

Alice nodded. "James has even given me space at his office down at the wharf so that I can accompany him to work each day. Although, once the baby arrives, I'll do so less. We haven't quite worked out all the pieces, but James is very supportive." Alice dropped a hand to her abdomen and the blessed bundle growing inside, then gazed at her friend. "I've been thinking. If the fire hadn't occurred, then we would never have become mail-order brides. We would never have met our dear husbands."

Beth stared at her in disbelief. "Leave it to you to find a bright spot in that awful blaze that ruined so many lives."

"But ours became better, so it is a bright spot. You can't deny it."

The kettle whistled. Alice stood and filled the teapot. "What of the other girls?" she asked over her shoulder.

"I recently received a letter from Lottie. She and Samuel are living on a ranch in Clear Creek, Oregon, and she's surrounded by cattle."

Alice laughed. "I'm sure she has much to say about that."

"No doubt. She said that Leora is doing well although she didn't know any particulars. And I still haven't heard from Judith. I'm eager to find out what happened after her groom died."

"As am I." Alice lifted the tray and indicated for Beth to return with her to the parlor.

"And although Lessie and Josie went to Utah Territory together," Beth continued, "Josie wrote and said her new husband had taken her to New Mexico." Beth pushed open a door so that Alice could enter the sitting room.

"Lessie must be terribly upset," Alice said.

"I imagine so."

Alice set the contents for afternoon tea on a table in the parlor as James and George entered, deep in discussion about fishing for pogies.

Beth settled across from her on the settee. "You must let me help you prepare supper, Alice."

"I'd be happy for your help, on one condition."

Beth watched her expectantly.

"No cabbage soup."

THE END

I'm so pleased you chose to read *Alice: Bride of Rhode Island*, and it's my sincere hope that you enjoyed the story. I would appreciate if you'd consider posting a review. This can help an author tremendously in obtaining a readership. My many thanks. ~ Kristy

American Mail-Order Brides Series

50 brides, 50 states, 50 books

* * * *

The American Mail-Order Brides series is a collection of sweet romances set in 1890 America. Beginning with *Lottie: Bride of Delaware* and ending with *Kitty: Bride of Hawaii*, each book features a state in the Union and showcases an unprecedented collaboration between 45 of your favorite western historical authors.

* * * *

Read the *Prequel* by Kirsten Osbourne for free.

Learn more about each story at newwesternromance.com.

Join us at our Facebook page - Facebook.com/AmericanMailOrderBrides/ - for updates and promotions.

About the Author

Kristy McCaffrey writes historical western romances set in the American southwest. She and her husband dwell in the Arizona desert with two chocolate labs — Ranger and Lily. Their four children are nearly all grown and out of the house. Kristy believes life should be lived with curiosity, compassion, and gratitude, and one should never be far from the enthusiasm of a dog. She also likes sleeping-in, eating Mexican food, and doing yoga at home in her pajamas.

Connect with Kristy
Website - kristymccaffrey.com
Newsletter - kristymccaffrey.com/Newsletter.html
Blog - *Pathways* - kristymccaffrey.blogspot.com
Facebook
 - Facebook.com/AuthorKristyMcCaffrey/
Twitter - Twitter.com/McCaffreyKristy/
Pinterest - Pinterest.com/kristymccaffrey/
Amazon Author Page
          -Amazon.com/Kristy-
          McCaffrey/e/B004NXSCNC/

If you'd love to connect with readers and authors in the western historical romance genre, please consider joining the Pioneer Hearts Facebook Group - Facebook.com/groups/pioneerhearts/. Lively discussions, author interactions, and members-only giveaways are guaranteed.

Read an excerpt from *A Westward Adventure* ~ a short historical western romance novella by Kristy McCaffrey

A Westward Adventure

Aspiring novelist Amelia Mercer travels from New York City to Colorado to aid an injured aunt. When the stage is robbed and her luggage stolen, bounty hunter Ned Waymire comes to her aid, acquainted with the harmless culprit and wanting to spare the boy. But Ned also seeks to impress the independent young woman. Amelia's wish to never marry, however, clashes with Ned's desire to keep her reputation intact. When a final bounty from Ned's past threatens their future, she knows that *A Westward Adventure* isn't just the title of her novel but the new course of her life.

Chapter One

Colorado
San Juan Mountains
May 1888

"Your name, miss?" The elderly town marshal, sitting at a desk across from her, watched her with a shrewd gaze at odds with his weathered and wrinkled skin, creases fanning the corners of his eyes. She found herself unable to look away from the sagging flesh, intriguing in its complexity, and she knew she'd have to write down a description as soon as she had a moment to herself.

"Amelia Mercer." Sitting ramrod straight on the wooden chair, she relaxed stiff fingers from the embroidered reticule on her lap and smoothed out her plaid wool traveling gown, the distress from the earlier shenanigans finally abating.

"What was stolen from you?"

"All of my luggage." Dresses, hats, gloves, linen handkerchiefs, a cape made of wool, several shawls, extra boots and shoes, and unmentionables — she didn't have one shred of clothing upon her arrival in the town of Laurel, except what she currently wore. A sigh of irritation escaped her lips. She hoped her aunt would be able to accommodate her until the hoodlums who held up the stage could be found.

"How many pieces?"

The door banged open behind her and she twisted to see what caused the commotion. A filthy man with hands cuffed behind him stumbled into the room, followed by a taller one. And while the much larger one was sweaty and a bit unkempt as well, his presence filled the room. His dark gaze caught hers. He was every bit the rugged western man she aimed to write about. His Stetson wasn't for show, dusted with dirt as it was. His attire spoke of days in the saddle, his boots and gun holster showcased a strong frame, his unshaven face proved that here in the west, men were men, and didn't hide it.

Amelia caught herself staring, only this time it had nothing to do with wrinkles.

Many fine men in New York City had courted her, but at twenty-two, her attention became more difficult to capture with each passing year. Were they simply too clean? The thought amused her.

I need to write these gems down.

"Lloyd Billings," the marshal exclaimed. "How on earth did you find him, Ned?"

"It's a long story, Ike. I beg pardon on the interruption, miss." The hale and hardy man nodded in her direction. "I'll just put him in the holding cell and return later to work out the details."

"Sounds good," the marshal replied. "Now, Miss Mercer, where were we?"

Reluctantly, she shifted her gaze from the finest specimen of man she'd ever seen to the wrinkly lawman.

"Please describe each piece of luggage and the contents," Marshal Ike said.

Amelia frowned as she attempted to concentrate, mumbling her way through the belongings contained in two trunks and one satchel.

"They stole it all?" Ike asked.

She lost track of the conversation as she listened to the rugged man locking the cell and walking to the door.

"I'll be back to collect the bounty." And with that, the compelling stranger was gone.

"You sure did bring a great many belongings with you," the marshal continued. "You plannin' to stay long?"

"Yes, as a matter of fact, I am. Theodora Thurston is my aunt. I've come to visit with her."

The marshal's eyes lit up, briefly smoothing the drooping skin. "You're Teddy's niece? Well, it's a pleasure to meet you, Miss Mercer. She's a fine woman. We hope she'll recover soon."

"As do I. I'd like to get along as soon as we're done. I've yet to see her."

"Of course. We're finished here. As soon as I know somethin' about the robbery, I'll let you know." He stood. "Let me escort you to Teddy's house. It's on the far end of town."

"I'd be most grateful." Amelia stood. "May I inquire as to who that man was?"

"Ned Waymire? He's a bounty hunter."

Amelia was certain her heart skipped several beats. She'd found the hero of her novel and wondered how she might encounter the gentleman again. She thought to ask the marshal, but he might think her forward, and she didn't want to embarrass her aunt. She'd have to find another way to inquire about Ned Waymire, Bounty Hunter.

She couldn't wait to get to the privacy of her room so she could describe the man of her dreams. Her *heroine's* dreams, she corrected.

* * * *

Ned dropped his horse at the livery, then stopped in at Laramy's Saloon for a shot of whiskey, or two. Catching up with Billings had been tedious and annoying and wholly satisfying. He only hoped that now he could, at long last, pick up Buck Mattick's trail. Lloyd Billings was a known accomplice of Mattick's. Four years ago, the scum had murdered Ned's pa. If it was the last thing he ever did, Ned would have justice.

He swallowed the liquor, enjoying the burn down his throat.

The marshal sure had a fine-looking woman sitting with him, her back starch-straight, her auburn hair swept up under a fancy hat, and an elegance that certainly pegged her as not from these parts.

Ned glanced around for Laramy's ladies. Maybe he'd been without a woman too long. The only one in sight was Lorna, and her red hair and mean countenance—although subtle—held little appeal for him despite her luscious assets. Truth was, none of the females, here or anywhere, held any interest for him. His restlessness of late had extended to the bedroom.

He'd just closed on the Parker place, so he could at least throw his energy into his new home.

He liked the sound of that.

He'd gotten the idea from his pal, Shep Sinclair, who'd done the very same thing last year.

Ned had always thought settling down only happened with a wife, but Shep had dug in roots and seemed content enough, and he still had no missus. So, Ned decided he'd give it a try, too. He liked Laurel. He liked Colorado. His pa had, as well. Staying here gave Ned a connection to the old man, and that seemed important.

But what about a wife?

The image of Miss Elegance lingered in his mind.

Damn.

He tossed back another whiskey, and pushed off to return to his current humble abode — a room in the home of Teddy Thurston.

* * * *

"What in tarnation are you doin' here?"

Amelia froze on the front porch, stunned speechless by the greeting from her aunt.

The woman glaring at her stood on crutches and despite her petite stature, filled the space like a roaring lion. Amelia took a step back.

"Teddy, this here is your niece," Ike said.

"Well, of course it is. You look just like your mama, Octavia. I just wasn't expecting you."

"I sent a telegram..." Amelia said, uncertain how to proceed.

Teddy sighed and shook her head. "I'm behind on my mail. My apologies. I wasn't prepared for company." She shifted so they could enter.

"I'll be on my way, ladies." Ike tipped his hat and scurried back down the steps.

Teddy made a frustrated sound, her gaze lingering on the marshal.

Amelia looked from her aunt to the lawman, then back. "Is he your beau?"

Surprise lit up Teddy's face, and Amelia couldn't help but smile. Her aunt was only human after all, and wouldn't gobble her up and spit her out behind the house.

"Well, I...hmm..." Teddy leaned on the crutches and moved into the parlor. "Let's not talk about me." She settled onto an ornate, but well-worn, sofa. "Please sit. Amelia, isn't it?"

"Yes, ma'am." Amelia untied the ribbon at her chin, removed her hat, and set it and her reticule onto another chair, then sat. Teddy leaned in and hugged her. The embrace was fierce, and for the second time Theodora Thurston stunned Amelia.

"It's mighty good to see you, dear," Teddy said. "How is my sweet sister?"

"She's well. It was difficult when Papa passed, but she keeps busy with her clubs and teas. She's quite the suffragette."

Teddy laughed. "I'm not surprised. Our mama embraced it with all her heart. Have you heard the story of the Seneca Falls Convention in '48?"

"Of course." Her grandmother, Sarah Thurston, only twenty-three years old and a young wife and mother, traveled to the first women's rights convention held in Seneca Lakes, New York with several friends. It had charged her with purpose for the female gender — one that she'd instilled in her own two daughters and her only granddaughter, Amelia.

"How is my mother?" Teddy asked.

Amelia's heart filled with love. "She's very well, too. You'd never know she was sixty-three. She's as robust and healthy as she was at twenty. Or, so she says."

"That's good to hear. I really must get back to New York one of these days. Maybe when this damn broken ankle heals."

Amelia couldn't hide the shock over her aunt's language.

Teddy hooted. "Dear, I'd apologize for my words, but you better just get used to them. I don't bend for no one."

Amelia's discomfort dissolved. Aunt Teddy had the sharp tongue and quick wit of all the Thurston women, and her resemblance to Amelia's mother was uncanny, although Teddy bore the mark of western living, in her practical split skirt and in her words. She'd left the family years before, when Amelia was but a child, and over time she'd become the center of extravagant tales. Amelia had been intensely curious of this female relative, who seemed to already be living the life that Octavia Mercer and Sarah Thurston fought so hard for back East. And she wasn't married, a state to which Octavia and Sarah had succumbed. Amelia was determined to be more like her legendary Aunt Teddy.

"How long will you be here?"

"I'd planned to stay at least three months," Amelia answered. "I've never been out West. It's such a grand adventure. I didn't want to waste the opportunity."

The front door opened and shut, and in the next instant, Ned Waymire filled the parlor entryway. As soon as Amelia locked eyes with him, he froze.

"Ned, I'd like you to meet my niece, Amelia Mercer." Teddy waved him into the room. "Amelia, this is Ned Waymire. He boards here. There's also another gentleman, but he's been away recently."

Mister Waymire removed his hat, revealing dark hair, and cleared his throat. "Pleased to make your acquaintance, miss." He stepped forward to take her hand.

The touch was warm, and his sun-darkened fingers overwhelmed her pale ones. As she smiled and nodded, she tried to ignore the tingling sensation that crept up her arm. Up close, he exuded even more strength than was apparent in the marshal's office.

A man who spent his days outdoors.

A man who called the earth his home.

Vivid blue eyes stood out on a sun- and whisker-darkened face.

He was the perfect western hero.

"I just saw you," she said, glad her voice sounded calm considering how her insides quivered.

"That's right."

He stepped back from her.

"You're not married, are you, Amelia?" Teddy asked.

"No, ma'am."

"Why, neither is Ned."

Heat suffused Amelia's cheeks. "I don't believe in marriage, much like you, Aunt Teddy." The words rushed out of Amelia. "Women don't need men to make their way in the world. Why, look at you! You've done quite well on your own."

"I've never been placed on a pillar," Teddy said. "What do you think of that, Ned? I'm a woman of example."

"I won't argue with that," Ned replied.

"Did you get Billings?" Teddy asked.

"Yep. You were right. He was in Old Man Hill's abandoned mine."

"I knew it." Teddy chuckled under her breath.

"Are you a bounty hunter, too?" Amelia asked.

Teddy cackled. "No, but I could be. Don't you think, Ned?"

"You'd outgun us all, Teddy."

Amelia sensed an affection between the two, and it warmed her heart, although this entire reunion with her aunt was far different than anything she imagined. She knew she had the first chapter of her new novel.

"I'll just be turning in now, ladies," Ned said.

Amelia, her cheeks still warm from being in the same room with him, met his eyes briefly then looked away in embarrassment.

What if he thinks I like him?

She imagined the type of woman he fancied was far from the likes of her. Why, he probably thought her a silly city girl. And he'd be right. But her mama had long taught her to be an independent thinker, to believe that a woman's mind was equal to a man's. Most of Amelia's writings had been social commentaries, addressing important issues such as the educational welfare of children, the plight of the homeless and less fortunate, and the lack of voice the average woman had within marriage. But in her heart, she longed to pen an adventurous tale of a woman who not only saw the world, but tamed a man in the process; who found love with an equal, inciting passion in her partner.

She hadn't told her mother she planned to write such a novel — she'd likely think it beneath Amelia — but her heart burned with the desire to share the story singing in her heart. Coming to visit Aunt Theodora had offered the perfect blend of adventure and inspiration.

Ned Waymire departed the room and his footsteps could be heard climbing the staircase.

That man was the epitome of adventure and inspiration.

Read 'A Westward Adventure' in the *Cowboy Kisses* anthology today. Available in Ebook at Amazon, iBooks, Kobo and Barnes & Noble. Also available in trade paperback at amzn.com/1507576501/.

46617196R00107